RAVEN SPEAK

Diane Lee Wilson

Margaret K. McElderry Books
New York London Toronto Sydney

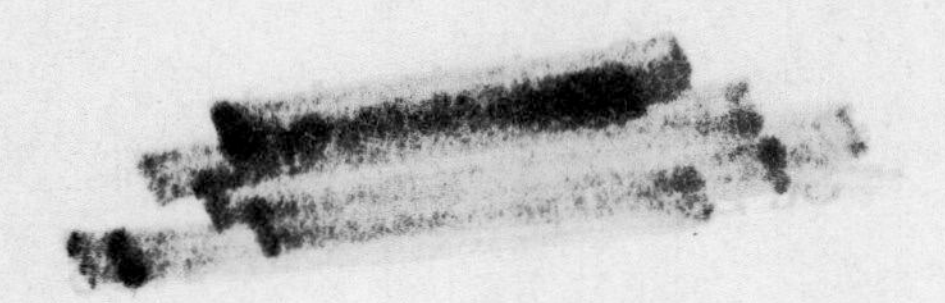

MARGARET K. McELDERRY BOOKS
An imprint of Simon & Schuster Children's Publishing Division
1230 Avenue of the Americas, New York, New York 10020

This book is a work of fiction. Any references to historical events, real people, or real locales are used fictitiously. Other names, characters, places, and incidents are products of the author's imagination, and any resemblance to actual events or locales or persons, living or dead, is entirely coincidental.

For information about special discounts for bulk purchases, please contact Simon & Schuster Special Sales at 1-866-506-1949 or business@simonandschuster.com.
The Simon & Schuster Speakers Bureau can bring authors to your live event. For more information or to book an event, contact the Simon & Schuster Speakers Bureau at 1-866-248-3049 or visit our website at www.simonspeakers.com.
Also available in a Margaret K. McElderry Books hardcover edition.
Book design by Paul Weil
The text for this book is set in Adobe Caslon.
Manufactured in the United States of America
0311 MTN
First Margaret K. McElderry Books paperback edition April 2011
2 4 6 8 10 9 7 5 3 1
The Library of Congress has cataloged the hardcover edition as follows:
Wilson, Diane L.
Raven speak / Diane Lee Wilson.
p. cm.
Summary: In 854, the bold fourteen-year-old daughter of a Viking chieftain, aided by her old and thin but equally intrepid horse and an ancient, one-eyed seer, must find a way to keep her clan together and save them from starvation.
ISBN 978-1-4169-8653-9 (hardcover)
ISBN 978-1-4169-8654-6 (pbk)
ISBN 978-1-4424-0249-2 (eBook)
1. Vikings—Juvenile fiction. [1. Vikings—Fiction. 2. Survival—Fiction. 3. Fortune telling—Fiction. 4. Horses—Fiction.] I. Title.
PZ7.W69057Rav 2010
[Fic]—dc22 2009018344

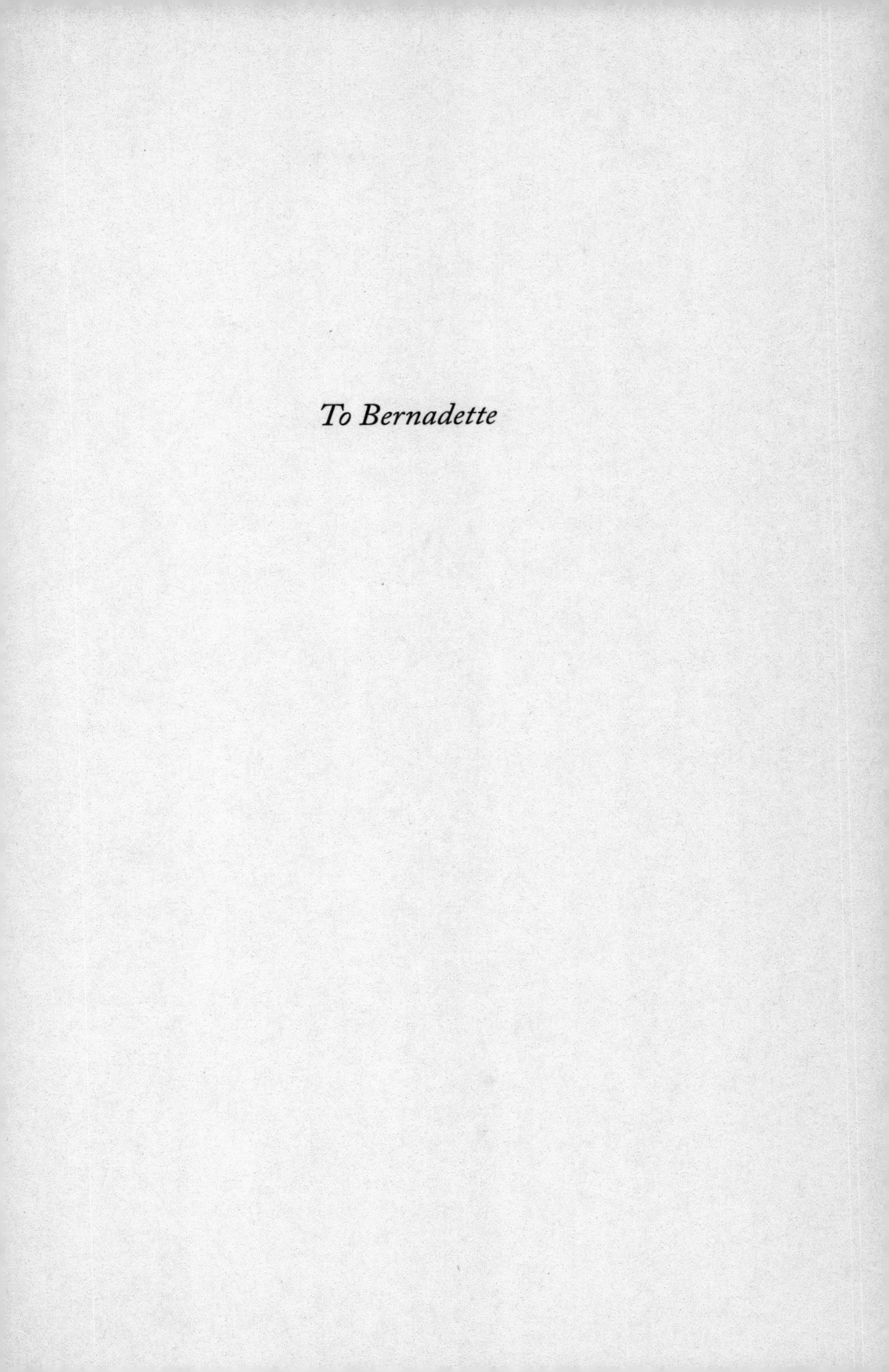

To Bernadette

EIN

In the pale light of a wintry morning seven men saddled their ship across bucking white waves. A girl stood alone on the shore. Stiff and silent, with her fingers clenched into fists and her eyes creased into flashing slivers of blue ice, she watched them go. The others of her clan, those that still lived at least, had long since shouted their fare-you-wells. But they'd left their crumbs of hope at the ocean's edge to shuffle back to the village, slump-shouldered and spiritless. The girl remained, staring rigidly at the horizon.

As dawn edged across the ponderous gray sky, the ship grew smaller and smaller. Its struggling flight was measured by the ocean's slow, rhythmic breath, a sucking inhale followed by a rushing exhale that darkened the shore. Spray misted the girl's face and beaded her brow. The anger bubbling inside her vibrated the glistening beads, and some shook loose to trace the bridge of her nose while others skated down her temple and crossed her hollow cheek. The trickling water surprised her and then, just as quickly, shamed her. *Don't you cry,* she scolded. *Don't you dare cry.* And to make certain she obeyed, she dug her nails into the flesh of both palms.

When the fogged horizon finally swallowed the ship, taking her father from her silently and completely, the vast ocean seemed to swell with a vicious pride. She kicked at a speckled stone. It stuck to the wet sand, cold and obstinate. Angrily she snatched it up and hurled it into the surf. Its noiseless scuttling did nothing to assuage her. So she threw another stone, and then another and another, heaving with all her strength and grunting like an animal until the dun horse behind her nickered his worry. That finally spun her round. Gathering up the reins, she threaded her fingers through his thick mane and flung herself across his back. She loosed her fury by drumming on his sides, and like the spark off a strike-a-light, he bolted. A sheet of airborne sand spattered the froth behind them.

Along the entire length of this westward-facing shore, black-green mountains plunged their ridged fingers deep into the sea. The clan's village was nestled beside a fjord that separated one mountainous thumb from a mountainous forefinger, but the girl and her horse galloped hard in the opposite direction. Across the narrow ribbon of sand they flew, soaring over splintered driftwood and dodging ropy mounds of rockweed. Like the dragon-prowed ship they danced through the churning surf, leaping and twisting and flinging themselves at their own horizon. All the way around the long first finger they galloped, past the fishing huts and ribbed boats humped in rows like so many sun-drunk seals, and then the fat middle finger, where a whale had beached itself two summers ago and closed its glassy brown eyes for the last time and now there wasn't even a bone left in remembrance, and on toward the neighboring finger. There she spied the silhouette of the ancient picture-stone with its weathered, mysterious carvings that she'd once paused to examine. But not today. When they'd rounded that tip of land and reached the shadowed fjord splitting it from the next, the girl realized how very far they'd gone—farther than they'd ever gone—and she fought the horse to a walk.

In wind-whipped defiance he shook his head. Trumpeting a blast of air that ricocheted noisily up the fjord, he let out a weak buck. Wondrous, really. In the barren days of this unending winter, when he was no more than dandelion fuzz on a skeleton, he bucked. That, at last, brought a smile to the girl's face, and she laid a chapped hand on his thin neck.

Rune. The horse she'd known all her fourteen winters, the one she'd learned to ride even before she'd learned to walk. Aged now, but still her daily companion and most loyal friend. The cold air spun his breath into dragon smoke that swirled around his hairy ears, but Rune didn't seem to mind; his head was up, eager. He'd been born to the cold.

Dropping the reins, the girl pulled first one foot and then the other up to the horse's withers, trying to rub some feeling back into her toes. Would this cruel winter never end? It was nearly Cuckoo Month now, and bitter winds still scoured a beach empty of life. She let her legs go slack, scratched the roots of Rune's mane, and sighed, but she didn't shiver. She'd never shiver. She'd been born to the cold too.

From her very first day, when she'd been ceremonially laid on a nest of fresh reeds at her father's feet, she had not cried; in fact, she'd not even shivered. How many times had he told her the story? All twenty-some members of their clan had gathered around the stone-ringed hearth after the night meal to watch him decide if she was worthy. As chieftain he could grant her life, assign her a name, and offer the clan's protection. Just as easily he could wave her away, and then the skald would have carried her out to the rocks at the ocean's edge and abandoned her to the biting winds and the hungry gulls.

"You never cried," he always began his retellings. "Both of your brothers mewled like orphaned lambs, but not you. You didn't cry, you didn't shiver, and you didn't even blink," he said, warming up to his part in the story. "You latched your round blue eyes onto me and stared so seriously, so boldly, that at first I didn't know what to do. Just ask your mother. So I scratched my ear, like this." And here he paused to dig a finger into his left ear. "And I looked at my ring, like this." He extended a hand to examine the engraved silver band. "And all the while you just went on staring at me like Jorgen the skald when he hungers for another piece of amber to carve his magic. I knew right then and there that you were no ordinary child, and I lifted you onto my knee. 'This is no ordinary child,' I said, and I cradled you in one arm like this," and here he always crooked his arm and looked down at his empty elbow, "and I sprinkled water from the fjord onto your round bare belly. 'She is to be called Asa Copperhair,' I pronounced, for from the beginning you wore a crown of gold-red hair that rivaled the firelight. And I gave you your first gift: a copper spoon."

That had been somewhere near midwinter in the year 854. And her father had been right: She was not an ordinary child—her name had lasted only three more winters. The girl, whom her mother had to drag by the wrist to help shell peas or knead dough or smooth clothes on the whalebone board, always managed to slip away the minute heads were turned. If someone took the time to chase after her, she could be found in the outfields picking small fistfuls of grass for Rune and the other grazing horses, or leading them to the mountain stream, or generally fussing over them until nightfall when, all by herself, she herded them into the byre with wildly flapping arms and a small shrill voice. If she didn't appear beside the hearth for the night meal, she knew someone would be sent out to the byre to unclench her fist from Rune's mane and lift her sleeping body out of the reed bedding. "So by the time you were four," her father went on, "I had to admit my mistake—which, as you know, is not an easy thing for me to do—and I had to gather everyone for another naming ceremony. Again I sprinkled the cold water from the fjord onto you, only this time I dribbled it on your head." He held his hand above her and mimed sprinkling water onto it. "And that time I got it right. 'She is to be called Asa Coppermane,' I said." And he'd given her a horse-headed comb carved from antler.

The two prizes, the spoon and the comb, still dangled from the chain fastening her brown woolen cloak, and she fingered them, remembering. As the fog receded she looked out to the ocean horizon again. The ship was indeed gone. Stung with regret, she shouted the blessing she'd withheld all morning: *"Fare you well!"* But the wind whipped the words back to shore and she knew her father would never hear them.

Her call elicited an annoyed *gronk* above her head, and she looked up to see a raven lifting off the cliff face. It had been picking through a last year's fulmar's nest and the sight made her stomach growl. How well she remembered snatching up newly laid eggs one after the other and sucking them down so fast that the sun-yellow yolks dribbled down her chin. Her mouth watered. For months now there had been only tasteless onion soup and crumbly flatbread stretched too far with dried peas and pine bark. Needles poked her stomach constantly. Would this winter never end?

While Rune nibbled at the gluey remains of something washed onto the shore, Asa followed the raven's flight. It circled overhead at first, eyeing her warily and *gronk*ing intermittently, then tipped its wings and flapped away. The cliffs flanking the fjord were so tall that the inlet's neck was cloaked in darkness. This would be the end of their ride.

She was just turning away when a movement caught her eye. Along the opposite cliff face farther up the fjord stood a figure with an arm outstretched, and the raven, as if summoned, spiraled downward to alight upon it.

In the moments that followed, time seemed to slow, and while Asa's heart thumped steadily, her breath caught in her throat.

They were watching her, the person and the raven both; she felt certain of it. She sat motionless on Rune, apprehension dragging a finger along her spine. But then the bird was drawn close and both figures melted into the dusk.

Odd. She'd never heard anyone in her clan speak of another settlement in the area. The next village was far to the south. Curious, she urged Rune forward a few steps, craned her neck, and squinted, but the pair had definitely vanished. Odd.

The ocean rumbled as a large set of waves rushed the shore. A freshening wind whipped peaks of white from the choppy waters, in turn cold gray and bronzy green, and she looked to the sky with new worry. The pale light was rapidly withdrawing, fleeing from low-hanging clouds that glowered with menace. Images of hurled stones sinking beneath the waves mingled with the last sight of her father's ship; no bigger than a stone it had seemed then, and she welled up with anger for those that had pushed him to such a foolhardy venture. It was the whispering that had done it, whispering that stirred doubts and suspicions, and the clan had listened with their bellies instead of their minds. Now, she feared, they'd suffer all the more. Gathering the reins, she looked again at the empty bird's nest, just a fringe of dried grass shivering in the breeze. If only summer would hurry.

TVEIR

Frost still rimed the wood planks of the byre door as Asa looped her fingers into the knothole. She threw her weight back in a succession of short jerks and it gradually came open, its cold hinges shrieking complaint.

A sour odor wrinkled her nose as she led Rune down the earthen ramp and into the dark, windowless shelter. None of the animals there greeted them; the cow merely flicked an ear, while her father's two horses swung their heads round for just a moment's dull gaze. Such a difference in a matter of months.

At summer's end, as was the custom, all of the clan's livestock had been divided into the weak and the strong. The small or sickly animals were slaughtered before winter could take its toll, and the healthy—three cows, five pigs, and twelve sheep, along with the horses—had been locked inside the byre. There'd been at least some hay waiting for them then, along with carefully doled out rations of oats and barley. But the food hadn't lasted, while the winter had.

One by one the remaining animals were slaughtered to feed the clan. It was a blessing almost, since they'd gone bony and shivering and in their final days their black eyes begged for relief.

These starving animals could only dream of such a fate.

She pulled a length of brown rockweed from Rune's shoulders and dropped it in front of the cow. The animal blinked and nosed the slimy strand with disinterest. She'd been spared all this time because she was pregnant, a seed of hope for the future. But the distended belly lolling over her folded legs seemed an absurdity, a bloated fungal growth sucking the life from its skeletal host.

The pigs were gone, along with their tasty chops and trotters, and the sheep, too, so there would be fewer woolen clothes for the clan this year. Already Asa's underskirt stopped well short of her ankles, and the tears across each knee had been clumsily sewn shut. Her overskirt hid these imperfections, though, and her cloak was well made. Sitting around the hearth fire at night, she could ball herself up inside it and nearly keep warm.

At the sight of the rockweed, the other two horses pricked their ears and nickered. Asa pulled another glistening strand off Rune and dragged it over in front of them. They dropped their heads in unison to examine the offering.

As always, she ran her fingers along the side of each horse, feeling for herself their deteriorating condition. Their thin, shaggy coats were so dry and bristly, so starved for nourishment. Beneath her fingers the horses' ribs pushed outward like barrel hoops. Her father had promised to bring grain if he found another clan with enough to share; otherwise the three animals, and Rune, would have to continue making do with the seaweeds she managed to scrounge from the shore or the inner bark she stripped from the pine trees. Her nails were shredded to the quick with that effort, and reddish resin mottled both hands. She didn't mind this as much as the very act of yanking the skin off trees and eating it. That made her feel desperate, no more than an animal. Indeed, every person in her clan was now sunk to being an animal, to scraping out a meager existence while waiting—hoping—to emerge from hibernation.

Although Rune was the smallest, he did the most work carrying her out and back through the icy weather, and so she removed his bridle and fed him the last whole length of rockweed. After a final pat on the neck, she checked the water level in the barrel braced in the corner. Unable to see anything in the gloom, she reached in. An icy skim sucked her fingertips to its surface, and she had to yank them free before using a nearby stick to stab the ice into floating chunks. Grabbing a pail, she slipped out the door and climbed the steep path to the stream that tumbled from the mountains. As always, she looked for signs of anything new, anything green and uncurling, *anything* to show that summer was on the way and that the land would once again nourish them. But the rocks were mostly bare, and as she climbed she felt she was the only living thing in all that bleak world: A silent forest cloaked the mountains rising above her; an endless, empty ocean stretched behind her; and an ominous gray sky, heavy with clouds, clamped down on the fjord like a shield of ice. What could raise its pale head here and sing of summer?

It was on her way back down the path that she finally noticed something different. The byre door was open, and a somewhat misshapen person was wedged into its gap: Jorgen the skald. He was the clan's storyteller, poet, and occasional prophet—a man she detested. And he was looking at the animals. Mindful of the slippery pebbles, she nonetheless quickened her steps. The splashing water cleared the pail's rim.

He heard her coming and spun. "What are you doing?" As if he couldn't see the pail for himself.

"Fetching water." She took a bold step forward, but he blocked the doorway with his twisted, turdlike body. Baths had occurred infrequently the last few months, but the skald had a peculiar odor that went beyond not bathing. It turned her stomach.

"You've not been fetching water all this time. Where did you disappear to after the ship's leave-taking? Your mother's been waiting for your report and you've worried her beyond any of my help."

If that was meant to hurt, it worked: His accusation drenched her with guilt. Her mother had been too ill that morning to walk to the shore to see off her husband and the other men. Yet Asa hadn't returned directly to her. Dwelling on her own worries, she'd gone galloping. "I went for a ride," she answered, and hastily added, "looking for food." Squeezing past him, she nodded toward the slimy weeds mouthed by the animals. His stench clung to her like a resinous film. Slowly, hoping he would leave, she rested the pail on the edge of the barrel and took her time pouring out the fresh water. But when the last drop had trickled into the barrel, she turned to find him studying the horses with the toothy greed of a wolf.

Her father, the clan's chieftain, had decreed that the remaining animals were not to be slaughtered. The pregnant cow was their only chance at milk and cheese and a future herd. And while eating horses was not out of the ordinary, these were her father's pride, a luxury he allowed himself. The red stallion was his and the bay had been a gift to her older brother. Rune had been intended for her other brother, but the impish creature had bucked him off with such abandon that for years Rune had worn a harness in the fields rather than a saddle on his back. Less than two years after Asa had been born, however, she'd discovered the horse dozing on the ground and clambered onto his back. They'd been inseparable ever since. She wasn't going to let anyone kill and eat him.

With that resolve in mind, she set her jaw and, giving the skald her iciest glare, moved past him. Claiming an authority that went beyond her fourteen years, she stood outside the byre door and waited for him to remove himself. Again she held her breath as he brushed past. What made him smell that way? Rotten onions? A bleeding tooth? Pee? She recoiled as he turned back and, still grinning, stepped right up beside her to help her shoulder the byre door closed. One behind the other then, heads bent, they hurried toward the longhouse. A stray, bitter wind raced up the fjord to snap at their heels.

Upon the stone door-slab, the skald hesitated and glanced back at the byre.

"The spruce trees are beginning to bud, I think," Asa said, hoping to prove that summer was coming, that wild cress and leeks would soon be in their future and in their stomachs. That they'd survive without having to eat the horses. "And I saw a fulmar's nest." Essentially true.

He looked down at her and grinned, showing wicked yellow teeth. "Did you now?" he said on a rush of noxious air. The odor fogged the entry until he turned and went into the longhouse. He scanned the room to see who was watching, then took his place beside the fire and sat, rocking.

The longhouse was as gloomy as the byre and nearly as cold. What had once been a snug shelter dancing with firelight and vibrating with people's laughter was now a sooty, smoke-filled hall. Peevish words were flung like gravel; lengthy silences hung in the air. The reeds covering the earthen floor had long been ground to dust. The soapstone dishes had run dry of whale blubber, so there was no light except for that coming from the fire glowing in the central hearth. In the early months of winter the iron cauldron suspended over the hearth had held rich brown stews of beef or mutton. Now, day after day, it kept a watery soup simmering beneath a gray foam. The flavor changed from bitter to greasy to burnt depending on what mushy vegetable was scrounged from the storeroom or what bony rodent was trapped, pounded to a paste, and stirred into it.

Asa hurried over to where her mother lay on a straw mattress pulled close to the fire. As wife of the chieftain, she'd be in charge of the clan until the men returned. So she'd left her private bed-closet at the south end of the longhouse and set up command by the fire's meager warmth. Secretly Asa wondered if it was all a mistake. Her mother, wrapped in a feather quilt overlaid with two sheepskins, could barely lift her head. How was she going to lead a restless clan?

As if sensing her worries, her mother reached out an arm to caress her daughter's cheek. "How is Rune today?"

Nothing about her husband leaving, nothing about every one of the able-bodied men leaving in a desperate venture to provide food. No, her mother would set aside her own worries to be a leader, strong in the face of the disaster that was engulfing them. "I found some rockweed for him and the others," Asa responded, "though we had to ride a long way. But when I carried water from the stream it looked like some of the spruce trees were beginning to bud. There were purple knobs on the ends of the branches."

With a weak smile, her mother tucked her arm back under her feather quilt and closed her eyes. "Tell me about your ride. What did you see?"

That was her way of asking for a story. In the monotonous, housebound months of winter, even insignificant events had to be told and retold, with ever more interesting details embroidered onto them, to help pass the time.

Asa recounted her ride around each finger of the mountain range, describing the ocean's changing colors, the ancient picture-stone that sprouted from the whale-nosed bluff, the weighty shapes of clouds in the sky, and ending with the raven and the strange figure. "I saw it land on a man's arm, but I didn't see a village anywhere. Does Father know about the people living there? Maybe they have food."

Her mother spoke with her eyes still closed. "I've never heard him speak of another village nearer than a day's sail away. Are you sure of what you saw?"

She thought. The fjord had been very shadowy, but yes, she'd seen the raven alight upon something that had to have been a person. She nodded. "Yes, I'm sure."

That brought her mother's eyes open. "Did he look evil—a raider or a pirate? Did you see his ship?" She lifted onto one elbow. "With the men gone we're easily taken. I'll have to do something, prepare. . . . I wonder if they saw your father and the others leave."

Ill as she was, her mother didn't need more worries. "Maybe it was just my imagination," Asa soothed. "The fjord was in shadow, and when the raven swooped into the shadows it looked like he landed on the arm of a person, but it was probably just a tree."

"You're sure?"

Her mother's eyes begged the answer, and so she gave it. "Yes," she replied, "I'm sure we don't have to worry about raiders."

And that, in essence, was also true. Why should they worry about raiders when they had nothing to be raided? The brutal weather had already stripped them of everything.

The months of late summer and early winter had been the harshest anyone could remember. Rain had fallen in torrents and the crops had become moldy. Then, almost without pause, the rain turned to hail and flattened the blackened stalks. What hay that could be salvaged from the mold was put up in the byre, but it was only a third of what was needed. Cabbages were stunted, pea pods mostly empty. The deer and elk climbed into the shelter of the high mountain forests, and even the gulls seemed to have flown to more temperate shores. In hard times the ocean had always provided plenty of food, but when the storms finally ceased, the fish, too, had apparently swum away, because time after time the nets were drawn in empty.

Needles pricked everyone's stomachs unendingly, and still the winter stretched on. Then, in the darkest days, an awful sickness had begun clawing its way through the clan. The room divided into those who turned their feverish faces toward the cold drafts whistling through the cracks and those who huddled beside the fire, unable to melt the frost that gripped their marrows. Hour after hour, day upon day passed when the clan's members sat in the dark, too ill to move, chewing on bark or vomiting it up. Movement ceased, and an entire day could go by before anyone noticed that a hand no longer twitched or that eyes stared unblinkingly at the rafters. No one was strong enough to dig a burial chamber; it was all anyone could manage to just roll the stiff body in a length of cloth, lay it on a plank, and carry it out to the smaller byre, the empty one, to wait in a frozen row with the others. Nine so far. Two of the shrouded bundles held Asa's brothers.

Was it the deaths of his sons that had driven her father out into a wintry ocean? Or the grumblings? She'd watched as he'd tried desperately to bolster the clan's spirits with enthusiastic plans for the coming summer: A new field would be cleared for more hay, a separate cooking house would be built for easier food preparation. Everything would improve. He openly complimented the women on their weavings and urged them to continue. He lapped up the soup that was served to him and pronounced it delicious even though everyone, including herself, could look into their bowls and see it was nothing but dregs.

But his smiles and optimism weren't enough. The cuckoo didn't come; the rains didn't cease; and the wool gave out. And hands couldn't weave hope out of nothing. The grumblings began that this was the chieftain's fault. He hadn't done enough—wasn't doing enough—to feed his clan.

So, thinner and sad-looking at last, he'd taken what few men were well enough and set out under stormy skies to find food or better land or possibly another friendly clan that had foodstuffs to share, though Thor knew they had little to trade. That left behind four women and five children, along with old Ketil, whose broken leg hadn't healed properly after his timber accident, and Jorgen the skald. Asa suspected he'd had a hand—and a tongue—in her father's ill-timed departure. While he'd always been kind to her, telling her stories and taking an interest in Rune and even carving a small likeness of him once as a gift, she seized every opportunity to escape him. There was something about him that made her skin prickle, something that wasn't right. And as she took up the comb to stroke her mother's hair, she warily studied the hunched man smiling to himself across the fire.

III
ÞRÍR

Jorgen held the smile on his face because she was looking at him and because it masked his real feelings. They were irritatingly strong feelings, feelings he couldn't quite control, and so he made himself smile while he sat thinking. And listening, always listening. And rocking.

She didn't fear him. That's what annoyed him the most. The others, even her pigeon-chested father, the clan's chieftain, could be made to move aside with a dark glance. It was a precious art, one he'd been polishing for many years now, and he wasn't about to let some child—a girl, no less—shrug that away.

He felt for and found the bear tooth amulet he had tied on a thong around his waist and kept next to his skin, hidden beneath his tunic. His father, the clan's skald before him, had given it to him, relating a belief about the amulet's power. He chuckled, allowing his smile to widen a crease. Funny how his father hadn't realized the heady power of his own position. For all the man's wisdom he'd never noticed how easily people could be influenced by a carefully worded compliment or chastened by a pointed rebuke. But Jorgen had; he'd hung in the shadows and watched people, all the while waiting for his father to die. And while he was waiting, he'd come to know each weakness and each want—and discovered how one could feed the other—for every member of the clan.

When his father had finally died—a terrible accident, really, bleeding to death all alone in the forest following a mishap with his axe—Jorgen had taken his honored position at the hearth fire. He continued entertaining the clan with the stories of his father and his father before him, but he recrafted the stories here and there to fill the clan's needs and to guide their desires. He told how great men rose up; how peoples came to be conquered; how the gods, in their pleasure, sought to aid humans—or in their anger, turned away from them.

Shaking his head, he released the amulet. They were like children, really, squatting with mouths agape, waiting to be spoon-fed the pabulum that was his stories. He'd nursed them well these many years, and they loved him as children love their father. And feared him, too, as children should a father.

All except one: this copper-headed girl, Asa. And that annoyed him. He reached for the amulet again, raked the bear tooth across the skin above his hip, relishing the prick, and released it. No, it more than annoyed him: It made the blood swell in his veins. The way she refused to step off the path when he approached made his chest hurt. Her stare, too direct, with gray-blue eyes flashing to every color of the ocean, made it hard to breathe. Sometimes she even argued a story's ending, as she had just the other night in front of all the others. It had infuriated him so completely that he'd lain sleepless till morning. Recalling it now lit a new fire beneath his skin, and he fondled the amulet. It wasn't right.

A torrent of raindrops began hammering the thatched roof, and he watched the dispirited members of the clan look upward. Worry soaked their faces, and he was quick to douse his smile, to look upward as well and be one with their misery.

The unusually foul weather of this past year had presented to him an unexpected opportunity. He'd always craved something more than he had, though up until now he'd not known exactly what that was. But as the nonstop rains rotted friendships, as the cold weakened resolve, he began noticing the chieftain's power eroding just a little. That made him think of things. And carefully, so very carefully, with all the cunning and patience of a wolf, he'd begun guiding the clan's thinking even more. He called up certain age-old stories of his father and embellished them. Or abbreviated them. He spoke ever more often of the gods' vengeance and the reasons behind it. Carefully, almost holding his breath, he deposited a suggestive whisper in one ear and a conflicting rumor in another until the clan members, blinded by misery upon misery, flopped about like fish in a net.

The chieftain had been surprisingly easy to sway. Over the past few weeks it had only taken a few private goads, along with a public appeal to pride and a veiled question of bravery, to send him off to sea in the worst of weather. And he'd taken the men with him, all but himself and old Ketil. Amazing, really, what a few well-placed words could do.

He let his eyes wander from the rafters to the empty looms set against the wall to the two figures directly across the fire. That left the chieftain's wife, leader of the clan in his absence, untended and alone. Her husband wouldn't return. Perhaps she didn't know it yet, but he did. The chieftain and his men would lose their battle with the gnashing teeth of a wintry ocean and find their graves in its depths. Their deaths would be crafted into a saga of bravery and added to the long list of others.

But here again was his problem: the chieftain's daughter, Asa, kneeling at her mother's head. His chest tightened. It seemed this girl was always in his way of late. He wouldn't have it. She'd have to be made to understand.

IV
FJÓRIR

All that morning winds lunged at the longhouse, raking the corner timbers and pummeling the turf roof. They withdrew, gathered breath, and charged again. Their crescendoing whistles frayed into stormy shrieks.

Asa sat cross-legged at her mother's side, tending to her. With one wary eye on the skald, she wiped a rag across her mother's feverish brow; she pulled the sheepskins off her when she moaned of heat, then tucked them back around her when she shook with cold; she brewed some yarrow tea, held the bowl to her mother's lips, and coaxed her to sip. All the while she tried hard not to think about the storm churning up enormous, violent waves.

But the more she tried *not* to think about them, the more she tried *not* to see her father's ship tossed wildly about by them, the more she envisioned the men's gaunt faces in the haze of smoke drifting beneath the rafters. Their mouths gaped for air as torrents of water washed over them. Fingers groped the blackness for the slippery hold of an oar. Again and again waves slapped them loose and hands flailed blindly for help that wouldn't come.

An icy breath prickled her nape. Her stomach soured. Was

it the awful images, or had the sickness finally wormed its way into her, too? She shook it off, flipped the rag on her mother's forehead to its cool side, and stared into the fire's orange glow.

Everything was going to be fine. The *Sea Dragon* was a good ship—small, yes, but sturdy, already the victor over many a rough sailing. And with her father at the steering oar, the men would be fine, just fine. They had to be.

As if mocking her confidence, the winds doubled the whistling fury they heaved at the longhouse, and somewhere on the mountains above them a loud snap preceded a long, ripping groan that ended in a crash. Mute faces exchanged a shared thought: As sturdy as the *Sea Dragon* was, its mast was no stronger than a tree. Nausea again swept over Asa, and she closed her eyes to mouth a prayerful plea to Odin to please, *please* quell the storm, at least until her father and the others could return home.

When she opened them she saw that Jorgen was inching his way around the fire. He came slowly, casually, speaking a word here, touching a head there, but all the while betraying his intent with half-lidded glances in her direction. She stiffened, understanding at once how the spring lamb must feel when, tucked into the tall grasses by its mother and instructed to remain still, it watches the wolf approach. Her jaw clenched as Jorgen sidled right up to her mother's mattress. It wasn't exactly the chieftain's seat left vacant by her father, but it was closer than he'd have dared if her father were here. She narrowed her eyes and gave him her best warning glare; but he seemed not to notice, or to care. He just sat, rocking on his heels and rubbing his misshapen knuckles, all the while stealing curious looks at her mother, who lay curled small with her eyes closed. A few of the others watched him with dull interest.

"Thor's hammering the heavens tonight, isn't he?"

He said it to no one in particular, but she found herself nodding. Her mother didn't respond at all, didn't so much as open her eyes. Asa saw that her shoulders were rising and falling with her quick, shallow breathing. Was she sleeping or only pretending? Jorgen wriggled a little closer.

"Or maybe it's Odin and his handmaidens, galloping their horses like our Asa here . . . only galloping them through the storm clouds to churn them to even greater fury." He looked around the room and chuckled, which sent a rotten plume of moist air rushing into the small space between them. "I've been thinking that maybe someone needs to prod those two stallions belonging to our absent chieftain into a battle. A good horse fight's been known to turn the weather good."

He was showing his ignorance. "There's no mare to spirit them," Asa snapped with more vehemence than she intended. "Besides, they're *starving*. How could they fight?"

Odd that he wasn't taken aback one bit. Odd that he smiled at her, though his lower lip, cracked and thin as it was, got stuck on one tooth and stretched like a slug before slipping free. "You're right, of course," he said, and when had he ever agreed with her? "I've seen the same with my own eyes."

He returned to his rocking, now fumbling with a fold of tunic at his waist. He reeked, absolutely reeked, of pee and something else that was both pungent and moldy, and the nausea that was kicking around her belly threatened to climb her throat. She snugged her cloak to her neck and tried to smell the cold sea air that still clung to it.

"Perhaps they have another purpose then."

That made her skin prickle. She had an instinctive urge to run out to the byre that instant—no, to grab Ketil's sword first and then run out to the byre—and to protect the horses with all the strength her arms could muster. No one was going to harm them.

He leaned even closer, which clamped her throat shut, and spoke in a confiding tone. "I'll have a word with your mother when she awakens, but I'm sure she'll agree that, with this storm so fierce and your father and the other men at sea so helpless, something needs to be done to alter the weather. And if none of the horses can manage to fight, then one of them, at least, can manage to die. The sacrifice of a horse, even this late, might appease the gods." An eager hammering of rain on the roof seemed to sound approval.

"We're not sacrificing any horses." Her mother spoke just as quietly as Jorgen yet with the undeniable authority of the chieftain's wife. Those few words, however, set her to coughing again, and as Asa reached out she noticed Tora whispering something to Astrid. The other woman, Gunnvor, silently cradled her sleeping son.

Asa stroked her mother's shoulder with concern and an

aching sense of helplessness. To her surprise, her mother reached up and removed her hand. She did it with a grim smile and gently, choking back another coughing fit. Lifting onto one elbow, her mother brushed the damp hair from her eyes and looked squarely at the skald. "You forget your place," she said. And even though her voice cracked, he did shrink back a little. "And my husband's wishes. We're not sacrificing any horses."

Jorgen turned up his palms in exaggerated innocence. "I was only thinking of the others," he said, loudly enough for everyone to hear. "Of everyone here who is hungry. The sacrifice of one horse, one aged horse, would at least provide some much-needed meat and might encourage the gods to provide good weather . . . and then good grass would follow so that the remaining animals could eat as well."

It was all Asa could do not to lunge at him, to clasp her hands around his scrawny throat and throttle him until he stopped twitching.

Her mother pulled herself all the way onto her knees, breathing heavily and looking pale and shaken. For the first time Asa realized the burden her mother carried. Though fever beaded her brow, she was forced by her position to paint on a brave smile. As the chieftain's wife, she had no choice but to fight through sickness and against doubt; whether she wanted to or not, she had to hold her chin steady and lead the clan.

Her hands were not quite as steady as her resolve, though, and Asa noticed her hiding them inside the sleeves of her tunic.

Jorgen did too. "Thank you for your advice, skald." She didn't speak his name. "But it is unwarranted and impossible. Summer will come; it always has. Asa says the trees are already budding, and I'll have her mount a bough over the door. Our men will be successful even in the face of this storm and will return with food." Her short speech crumbled into another coughing spasm, and Asa couldn't help but lay a concerned hand on her mother's shoulder again, though once again it was lifted away. "Now then," her mother continued when she'd composed herself, "Astrid, I'd like you to add another handful of dried peas to the soup cauldron, and an onion or two if there are any left." The woman rose and headed for the storeroom. "Gunnvor, how is Engli faring? Bring him here, closer to the fire. Ah, you've grown even since yesterday," she said when the blinking boy had been laid across the foot of her mattress. She bundled one of the sheepskins around his feet. "Such a strong boy. Ketil, there's a draft coming from somewhere over there near the door. Can you do us all the favor of stopping it up somehow? Careful now, mind your leg." Astrid returned with a small bowl of dried peas and a bruised onion and showed them to her. "Good. Now chop up that onion as fine as you can to spread the flavor. Can we stretch the flour even further with a little more pine bark?" Astrid nodded. "Fine." She looked across the fire to the woman who'd begun the whispering. "Tora, I have a silver ring pin that would be perfect for that cloak you're near to finishing—and don't you worry, I've told my husband to bring more wool along with food. Asa, here's the key to the chest, will you fetch it for me? It's the one with the copper inlay."

Asa climbed to her feet and went to the sleeping chamber she shared with her parents. Her mother's offer was generous, yet at the same time seemed more of a bribe than a gift. Is that what it took to lead? Did her mother have to buy the dispirited clan's support with kind words and gifts?

She pulled the heavy wooden chest away from the corner and knelt to fit the key into its lock. They weren't a rich family by any means, but her father was a clever trader and over the years had brought back many small adornments for her and her mother. When she lifted the lid, though, she saw that the chest had been emptied of nearly all of them. The set of four fragile drinking glasses were still cradled in their wool, but in the bowl that had once held handfuls of colorful glass beads only a pair of milky gray ones rolled around forlornly. One of her favorite amulets, the iron one molded to look like a tiny hammer, was gone from its necklace, and at least two of the carved bone combs were gone from their tray. Even her father's prized arm ring, heavy silver engraved with proud-necked horses, was missing. He wasn't wearing it when he'd left. Had he taken it for trade? Or worse, as the dismal days of winter had stretched long, had he been forced to give gifts as well?

She found the ring pin her mother wanted, closed the chest, and locked it. The ornament lay cold and sharp in her hand, an ugly feeling that outweighed its beauty. Could no one just say this is right or this is wrong and have others believe it? Did there always have to be coddling and persuasion? Were they really such children?

Upon her return she saw that Jorgen had retreated to the other side of the fire to crouch in an awkward fashion, still watching them with hungry interest. She placed the ring pin in her mother's clammy palm and felt her fingers tremble as they closed over it. Sunken into the purplish hollows of their sockets, her mother's eyes appeared unfocused. Her gaunt cheeks had a waxy look, like the skim on a hard cheese. Was she really well enough to make decisions for the clan?

"You should lie down, Mother," she said, and for the third time that morning she placed a hand on the woman's shoulder and tried to coax her onto her mattress.

The bony fingers that grabbed her wrist this time had all the strength of a gyrfalcon. "This is no time to be lying down," her mother scolded under her breath, and Asa saw that there was yet a small fire beneath the watery eyes. "For any of us." The talons dug deeper. "You must keep a close eye on those horses. Especially Rune."

She nodded, her heart suddenly racing. Then she knelt beside her mother and watched her press the ring pin into Tora's palm, an unspoken sealing of allegiance, and watched the skald watching them, and bit her lip until it bled.

The morning passed with little activity and even less talk and at midday, reassured of her standing, her mother allowed herself to lie down on her mattress and sleep. Asa took that opportunity to hurry out to the byre to see how the animals had weathered the storm. She half-expected the skald to follow her, but he'd also stretched out on his mattress and only twisted his head to watch her go.

The air was cuttingly cold, though patches of brilliant blue peeked between scudding clouds. The narrow stream, now muddied and swollen past its banks, roared eagerly downhill to the fjord. She looked across the choppy waters and out toward where the sea's expanse of glistening green rose to meet a newly rinsed sky. All around her the world sparkled, and that stirred in her a sense of hope. Remembering her mother's wishes, she broke off a spruce bough and mounted it above the longhouse door. Its keen fragrance stirred her. As poorly as the day had begun, things seemed to be heading in the right direction now.

Tugging the byre door open delivered a fresh shower of rain from the roof's overhanging turf. It also let in a cold gust that riffled the hairs on the four shaggy animals. The dim light showed that the leaves had been stripped from the ropy strands of rockweed and that the cow had moved to the far corner of the byre and was now lying there.

Rune climbed to his feet and shook himself off. Although age had dug thumb-size hollows above each eye, he still wore the inquisitive expression of a much younger horse, and that made him appear to be smiling. Ears pricked, he ambled over to bump his broad head against her arm. She scratched his poll and rubbed the insides of his furry ears, all the while knowing that wasn't truly what he wanted.

"I know, I know," she said. "And I'm sorry. I'm as empty as you are."

He turned away, his black and silver tail chest-high to her. That made her smile because it wasn't a rebuff but a simple demand for more scratching. "All right, that much I can do." And she dug her fingers into the sloping planes of his hindquarters and ran them up around the dock of his tail and then down each thigh, scratching hard. Rune stretched his neck and wriggled his lips with pleasure.

"The storm has probably washed up some more seaweed," she said when she'd finished. "We'll head out tomorrow and bring some back, all right?" Rune nodded his head and shook all over again, quite as if he understood.

Although she didn't have the same bond with the other horses, she took the time to scratch their withers and rub their ears. It wasn't food, but it was something. It helped to ease the suffering when someone cared, didn't it?

Squatting beside the pensive cow, she laid a palm against the animal's swollen belly. Deep under the coarse, curling hairs she found warmth. She waited, watching her own breath cloud the air and disappear, cloud and disappear, as rhythmic as the ocean. She slid her hand lower and waited some more. A steady *drip, drip* from the rafters to a puddle on the byre floor measured the cold passing of time. Finally, there it was: movement. The promise of new life, of summer's return. The grass would grow long, and the horses and the cow and her newborn calf would all grow strong on it. Life would continue.

But even as she was shouldering the byre door closed, the clouds were pinching away the blue. Intermittent pellets of cold, hard rain chased her back to the longhouse. And the stubborn wintry storm began gnashing its teeth with renewed fury, as if it were as hungry as they and was coming for them, too.

V
FIMM

"Jorgen."

After so much silence the rasping call from the wife of the absent chieftain jerked everyone's head up, including his own. He abandoned the repair he'd been trying to make to his rotting left shoe, stuffed his foot into it, and again made his way around the fire. This time, because he'd been summoned, he didn't pause to talk with anyone.

It gave him a shiver to boldly squat in the empty place at her side, the chieftain's seat. As his elbows met his knees, his heart quickened. She, too, was breathing with some effort, her chest rising and falling beneath her tunic, but it wasn't shared excitement. The sickness that had crawled through the nostrils and mouths of so many clan members and splatted out the bowels of the now dead ones had wormed its way deeply into her. He could almost warm his hands in the heat radiating from her feverish body.

Stop. He dug for and found the bear tooth and pressed its point steadily into his flesh. He bowed his head beneath this discipline and tried not to wriggle. "Yes?"

"We need a story," she said.

He lifted his eyes, by chance catching the daughter's suspicious expression. Deftly, careful to conceal any emotion, he slid his gaze back to the mother. The chieftain's wife—no, the chieftain's widow, he reminded himself—hadn't bothered to look at him at all as she spoke. Fully under the spell of the fire's dancing orange embers, she stared blankly, unblinkingly. "But it's not yet nightfall," he countered. "Don't you agree that stories are best saved for the evening?"

"Look around you," she said in a husky voice only a few could hear, "and prove the time."

She was right, of course; the longhouse slumbered in a cold, smoky gloom that belied dawn or dusk, day or night. Except for the copper-headed girl and one or two children and, oddly enough, himself, its remaining inhabitants were either too sick or too dispirited to move about. They hovered near their mattresses, perpetually half rising, half sleeping. There was nothing to reach for. Every waking breath seemed to deny hope.

The woman gathered herself and struggled onto one elbow, no doubt to hurry his answer, but instead triggering a spasm of coughing. It was a thick, swampy cough that drew her fists to her chest and flung her onto her back. The girl bent close, holding a bowl to her mother's lips. He watched the liquid dribble down the woman's chin, watched her shove the bowl away and push herself upright once more, bracing on one shaky arm. She was a tough one, he had to admit. Slowly she swung her head round to look at him, breathing hard, fighting the cough that convulsed in her throat. But he knew she was no match for it. And he was right. The cough exploded in her and from her and she doubled over again, helpless. The girl murmured something. Setting both hands on her mother's shoulders, she coaxed her to submit, to lie down and to give in, and his chest swelled with the possibilities.

The girl wasted no time at all in fastening her own eyes on him, eyes that stormed like the ocean's blue-black waves. "*Will* you tell us a story?"

Such insolence! That hot feeling raced beneath his skin again. How dare she, a child, command a story from him as if he were no more than a leashed dog? This was not how things were going to be.

Only now was not the time to chasten her, not with all the others watching. For now he had to store his scythe and plant another seed. He felt his lips widening into an agreeable smile. "Of course," he replied, "of course."

And he held his face in that ridiculously agreeable smile, his lips stretching thin, while he searched for the appropriate story. None of his father's stories was exactly right, he knew, none of them would hand to him what was so deliciously close to being in his grasp. He'd begin with a familiar one, though, then craft his own ending. And even as he was forming the plot in his mind the words came flowing out of his mouth. He heard them following one another so smoothly, so orderly, that no one could say this wasn't one of the time-honored, wisdom-filled tales of his father and his father before him.

VI
SEX

Asa only half-listened as she ladled water into the shallow washing bowl and carried it with still-trembling hands toward her mother. She'd questioned the skald before, even argued with him in good spirit, but she'd never taken it upon herself to order him to do anything. That was her father's right and, in his absence, her mother's. But she'd gone ahead and done it, and now he was angry. She knew so by the angle of his jutting chin and the flush of color across his cheek, color that seeped all the way down through the bristly hairs of his short beard.

Well, what of it? He was the one who'd overstepped bounds. As the chieftain's daughter she'd *had* to act and, kneeling beside the bowl that she'd placed behind her mother's head, she resolutely gathered a long hank of the oat-colored hair and swished the dirty strands through the water. Her mother murmured appreciation. Knuckles clenched to white, Asa wet the comb and pulled it firmly across the pale scalp.

The story Jorgen had begun was about a man wandering alone through a forest in the darkness of an unending winter. She knew the story; she knew them all, in fact. This one had several variations, but by the end the man—forever unnamed—always learned a lesson and found his way home.

"For all of his years this man had been wandering." In a deepened voice the skald meted out the familiar words with restraint, skillfully creating a sense of mystery once again. "But he was searching for something which he couldn't name. The winter winds howled in the man's face and the snow piled on his back. Yet day after day, year after year, he wandered. Until one morning, one cold wintry morning just as dark as every other, a woman rode out of the forest. When she appeared to this man the winds calmed and for one breath the sun blazed.

"This woman," he related, "this *beautiful* woman, was dressed in every shade of blue." Here Jorgen began speaking with infectious wonder, his nimble hands sculpting an image out of thin air. In spite of herself, Asa's combing slowed. "She was dressed in blue because she was a seer and knew the future. Her linen tunic had been dyed the color of ripe bilberries"—how lightly he pinched an invisible one between his thumb and forefinger before popping it on his tongue and swallowing in delight—"and her woolen cloak was the same shadowed hue as a swallow's feathers." His hands cut graceful arcs through the air as his fingers fluttered: small birds crisscrossing the sky. "The hems of both garments sparkled with blue glass and clear crystal beads created in a far-off land. Even her shoes, fashioned from the softest sealskin, had been dyed a dark blue and embroidered with blue and silver threads." A whistling sigh of envy escaped Tora, causing two of the younger children to giggle. Jorgen silenced them with a warning glare before continuing. "She came to this man riding on a white horse. 'What is it you seek?' she asked. He didn't know how to answer because a man can find himself ever so hungry, but if he has never tasted honey, for example, how can he say, 'It is honey for which I hunger'? So he said, 'I seek to stop wandering. I seek to not shiver. I seek to be other than alone.'"

Something poked at Asa. The words were slightly different, weren't they? Had anyone else heard a change? She scanned the room, noting the clan's slack jaws and unblinking eyes. Sorcerer that he was, Jorgen held them in thrall. But not her. She wet the comb again and listened more carefully.

He told how the woman walked with the man so that he wouldn't be lonely and how she helped him build a house of stone, wood, and turf so that he needn't wander. Nothing alarming in that. Her mother gave a sudden shiver, though, and Asa was quick to slide the bowl aside and wrap her wet hair in a thick cloth.

"Then one stormy day this man said, 'I am still cold. I am still hungry. Will it always be winter?' But even though the woman who had come to him was a seer, she didn't answer his question. She tended the fire and held the man to her breast and that is all she could or would do. Night after night the winter winds whistled through the trees and shook the snow from their branches. The wolves howled and the ice groaned and the forest slumbered in shadows as black as pitch.

"One night, when the man left his house to gather some

wood, the woman's white horse appeared to him from out of the forest. 'I can make you warm,' it told him. 'I can feed you. And I can bring summer.'"

Asa froze.

"'Take my blood,' the horse said, 'and scatter it on open ground. And take my bones and grind them into the dirt. And take my skin, emptied of all its worth, and mount it on a wooden frame at the edge of your new field so that all who see it will know what a gift I have given you.'"

Jorgen spoke rhythmically, almost soothingly, weaving his poison so deftly into the fabric of his story that no one would question it. Except her. She knew now his intentions, and she narrowed her eyes and saw him for the enemy that he was.

"And this man, who was a dutiful man," he continued, "did as the horse instructed. He picked up his axe and in one stroke he slew the horse. And he took the horse's blood and scattered it on the fields, and he ground the horse's bones into the dirt, and he mounted the horse's white hide on a wooden frame. And, lo! Before three days had passed the skies turned as blue as the woman's shoes and the sun shone as brightly as the crystal beads on her cloak and the man was warmed. Grass sprouted as high as his knees and the birds laid their eggs and the man was fed. Summer had returned."

The skillful hands at last came to rest in the skald's lap, the fingers humbly laced together. The weaving was done. The finished piece hung in each imagination, awaiting response. Jorgen allowed himself a modest smile as his shoulders twitched with the pleasure of his performance. The cocksure glance he sneaked toward Asa told something else altogether. He must have seen the horror in her eyes, because he looked away in the next instant and made a pretense of clearing his throat. Then he sniffed twice—quickly—rubbed his dripping nose with the heel of his hand, and chuckled.

"It seems that I probably should have told that story at the beginning of winter," he said, shaking his head and chuckling again. "A sacrifice then would surely have hurried summer's return; by now we would have had good weather and good grass." He shrugged meekly, pulled off his hat, and scratched the back of his head, then replaced the hat and stole another glance at her.

This was a game to him. Right in front of her he was inciting them to kill the horses and he was enjoying himself. Her chest hurt. The air rushing in and out of her nose burned.

Turning his attention to the others, he spread his oh-so-magical hands in humility. "It truly is my fault," he said, and his own nod encouraged agreement. "There are so many stories to remember, you see, so much wisdom from my father and his father before him. Yes, I was forgetful." There was the slightest of pauses, a subtle shift in his posture and stronger inflection in his tone. "Though forgetfulness"—he spoke very carefully now, very clearly—"is not to be confused with selfishness; it is selfishness that angers the gods, keeping for human use what isn't theirs."

There it was. He'd tossed the red-hot spark onto the kindling.

Old Ketil was the first to catch fire. He thudded his walking stick on the dirt floor for attention. "Is it too late for a sacrifice?"

Jorgen started to glance at Asa, caught himself, and pulled back. "We-e-ll," he said, drawing out the word to show full consideration of Ketil's question, "the damage, I fear, has already been done. You have only to look at our miserable existence. I don't know if the gods have any more interest in us, but . . ."

He was herding them off unchallenged. Someone had to do something. Asa looked to her mother and even touched her shoulder with enough force to waken her, but there was no response. The thin pale lids closed over her eyes didn't so much as flicker. Panicked, Asa found herself boldly chastising Ketil on her own. "My father forbade that the horses be killed," she said sharply. "You'll do well to remember that. Or the cow. They're all we have left."

Ketil's beard quivered and he blinked with indignation. Pursing his lips, he stamped his stick again. "But our situation is worse than your father ever expected. Now he's off to do what he thinks best—"

"It isn't what *he* thinks best but what you all *told* him was best."

Tora, of all people, joined his argument. "Whatever the reason for his going, the point is that he's not here and we need to do something." Asa went stiff. How could the woman take her mother's silver ring pin and then say such things? "In his absence—"

"In his absence my mother makes the decisions for us all."

Every eye in the room now fell on her mother, lying motionless on her mattress, apparently asleep and unhearing. Asa sensed their doubt. This was no leader, they were thinking. Her heart pounded.

"We will wait for her decision then," Jorgen pronounced, and that shoved her back on her heels. Why was he suddenly retreating? His furrowed brow was merely a transparent display of sympathy. "I suppose all we can do is wait. As the animals wait. As the insects wait." His gaze fell to the emptiness of his lap. Fiddling with something inside his sleeve, he began mindlessly humming a familiar line from a song of farewell. That released the others to whisper among themselves, or stretch out on their mattresses, or close their eyes and wait, insectlike.

Time passed with the room in suspension and Asa hardly able to breathe. All the while Jorgen kept humming, and while he hummed he lifted his head and leveled his heavy-lidded gaze at her. No one could say that his smile wasn't gentle, that his face wasn't full of concern for her and her sick mother. But the eyes lurking beneath that brow were neither gentle nor concerned. They glinted with the cold bite of death. And for the first time in her fourteen winters, Asa shivered.

VII SJAU

Asa dragged her own mattress to her mother's side that night, determined to keep one watchful eye on her and the other on Jorgen. From where she lay she could just see the two rumpled mounds formed by his blanketed feet, and she wordlessly focused her bitterness in his direction. She suspected it was Rune he wanted to kill—he was the oldest of the three horses—and her teeth ground together until she was forced to unclench her jaw and look toward the rafters. If she hadn't been needed here, Asa knew she'd be passing the night in the byre—that night and all the nights that followed, protecting the animals from Jorgen's demonic hunger.

Somewhere on the other side of the fire Ketil mumbled and sighed. Beyond Asa's head Gunnvor crooned to little Engli to soothe his sick whimpers. The flames burned lower and lower, and sleep gradually settled over the others; the coughing quieted, the sniffling eased. On any other night it would be easy enough for her to fall asleep, but Asa held herself rigidly awake. She turned and gazed long and hard into the rippling crown of orange flames without seeing them, but all the while nurturing their burn inside of her. Only when an ashy branch fell apart with a pop and a hiss did she startle back to the present, uncertain how much time had passed. In the room's silence she had a sudden, clear sense that Jorgen was lying awake too. Thinking about her.

That made the hairs on her skin lift up. Not wanting to—and scolding herself against it even as she pushed onto one elbow—she peeked across the flames.

Surprise gave way to alarm and abhorrence as she caught him peeking across the fire at her. Flushed with humiliation, she flattened herself on her mattress. She knew he lay down too. Again her chest heaved. What had he been doing?

The double quick thudding of her heart measured the night's progress after that. Like a hawk she pinned her eyes on Jorgen's blanketed feet, watching them shift restlessly, slanting east and then west and much, much later, collapsing to one side and falling still. Untrusting, she kept watch. The longer the blanket remained motionless, though, the steadier her heart beat until, finally, she allowed herself to stretch a little and roll onto her back.

She sighed, acknowledging her exhaustion. So much had happened in one short day. Her thoughts tumbled over the events like water rushing over stones. She mused about the *Sea Dragon*'s departure (and optimistically mouthed a blessing for its safe return); she thought about her ride on Rune and where she'd go tomorrow to scout for more rockweed; she pondered the raven and the strange person she might have seen. Whenever she felt the warm haze of sleep attempt to creep across her, she turned her head toward the skald and reignited her determination to protect both her mother and the horses.

Odd, wasn't it, the way he'd deliberately incited the clan to sacrifice a horse, then pulled them away from the idea, saying they'd have to wait like insects. She sniffed. There in the middle of the night, though, with the damp cold hovering over her body, she began to feel like one, like an insect burrowed deep within the black earth, waiting for the warmth of summer. But did summer always come for such creatures? Or did they die waiting?

It was awfully quiet now—no rain, no wind. The longhouse seemed to take the form of a living thing huddled in the dark, holding its breath to listen for something coming out of the night. Curious, she held her own breath and listened. Nothing unusual. A muffled rustling as Gunnvor shifted on her mattress. The pinging *drip-drip* of water from a leak in the roof. The annoyingly whiny whistle of Jorgen's snore. At least he was asleep.

But then she heard something else: an indistinct sound, far, far away in the skies. She wished she were outside so she could hear better. She held her breath again, lifted up, and listened. There it came: a faint, teasing cry. As heady as the fragrance of crushed tansy came the steady honking of grey geese announcing their return. Summer! Summer *was* finally coming!

Curling happily onto her side, she snugged the blanket to her chin and smiled. Warmer days lay ahead for certain, and with them green grasses, watercress, milk, and butter. In her mind the seas calmed and the fish began swimming in silvery schools back up into the fjord. The deer and elk picked their way down from the mountains. Across the hillsides yellow ladyslippers sprouted with abandon, nodding in the sun. She pictured her father's ship sailing up a friendly fjord to the greetings of a welcoming people. As the boat's hull scraped the shore a draft of cold air brushed her cheek, nudging her awake.

The room was still dark and mostly quiet, save for the monotonous *drip-drip* behind her. The fire had gone to coals. She let her sleepy gaze wander the shadows, identifying the baskets, the barrels, the bundled fishing net and coiled ropes, the legs of the bench, the sleeping forms of the others on their mattresses. She couldn't see Jorgen's feet and rose on her elbow to check his mattress. Empty.

That shot her upright. She scanned every corner of the room. He was gone. All the while her mind was backtracking over the sounds she'd heard in her dreams and identifying them differently, not as the boat hull scraping, but as the door opening and closing. He'd gone to the byre!

Scrambling to her feet, she searched for a weapon. The knife Astrid had used to chop the onion lay on the bench and she tiptoed over and around the sleeping clan to retrieve it. As quietly as she could then, her heart trying to tug her along faster, she slipped through the door and into the night.

The air was freshly cleansed, crackly with cold, and filled with the sound of rushing water. Streams, cataracts, rivers, and waterfalls echoed their frothy thunder through the mountains. Moonlight etched ripples across the glistening expanse of the fjord. She looked toward the byre. The muddy path glistened with a frosty sheen but the black footprints led to the smaller, empty byre where the clan had laid the dead bodies awaiting a summer burial. With her skin prickling—from the cold she told herself, not fear—she hurried up the path.

The door to the small byre hung ajar and for a breath she wondered if living hands had done that or if a *draugr*, one of the walking dead, had shoved it open. She thought of Bjor, ill-tempered enough when he was alive, always shouting coarse names at her for galloping away from his advances; she'd hate to meet up with him now, when his groping hands would no doubt be swollen to twice their size and strength. The skim of frost crunched ever so slightly beneath her feet and only too readily she slowed her approach. When she laid a hand on the door at last, her heart was climbing her throat. Swallowing hard, she peeked inside.

A rotting stench assaulted her nose as her eyes adjusted to the darkened interior. Jorgen was there, all right, on his knees, though she couldn't tell what he was doing. Praying over the shrouded bodies? As the darkness solidified into various shapes and silhouettes, she watched him flatten and sweep his hands along the ground. Some sort of magic ritual? No, that wasn't it; he seemed to be looking for something. Nose almost to shrouded nose, he reached under the crossed timbers that lifted the bodies clear of the ground and dragged out a cloth-wrapped bundle. With a childlike gurgle of pleasure he sat back on his haunches, hastily unwrapped it, and lifted it to his face. He was eating it! A morsel fell to the floor, and with the quickness of a cat he pounced on it and stuffed it into his mouth.

Surely pressing a fist to her stomach hadn't made a noise, but he suddenly stiffened, as an animal does when it realizes it's being watched. He glanced toward the door. Seeing her, he climbed to his feet. His height seemed to exceed his usual stature.

"There's enough to share." It was an eerily pleasant invitation.

"Then let's share it with everyone."

He chuckled. "There's not that much. But I do have something for you." As he walked toward her a rich, moldy odor preceded him. She clutched a fold of her cloak, prepared to run. The moonlight that spilled over him at the byre's entry cast his face in sharp relief. The wart on his nose bulged larger, the bristling hairs in his nostrils glistened with icicles of frozen snot. His thin lips had a peculiarly rosy color, as if he'd been sucking hard on something cold. What most grabbed her attention, though, was the crumbling chunk of pale cheese he offered on his palm. Her mouth flooded with anticipation.

"Take it," he said. "No one needs to know."

Her stomach joined her mouth in clamoring for a taste of the nearly-forgotten treat. *Just a bite. No one needs to know.*

But Jorgen would know. And that would tie them together in a way she couldn't endure. Gazing hungrily at the chunk, she shook her head. She swallowed her saliva, ignored her panging stomach, and demanded, "How could you hoard this food for yourself? The children are starving!"

"It's not that much," he argued. "A bit of cheese, some hazelnuts. I had a couple of eggs at one time but something got to them and ate them before I could. And there was some cod I'd dried myself." His own pride was hanging him.

"Then let's get it to them now. Let's wake them up."

His fingers closed over the cheese. "No. I warned all of you this would be a bad winter, including your father. Didn't I warn you? At least *I* prepared for it."

She remembered no such warning, though she did recall Tora counting and recounting the cheese rounds one day in the storeroom and, upon finding young Helgi and Thidrick playing a hiding game there, charging them with the loss of one whole cheese. Though they'd pleaded their innocence in tears, her father had punished the boys by making them haul enough water from the stream to fill every barrel in the longhouse.

Sensing a hesitation, Jorgen teasingly lifted the cheese toward her nose again.

"Bastard!" She pushed his hand away, accidentally revealing the knife she carried.

"Ah, so it's meat you're wanting. Well, I can serve that up for you as well." But in the same instant that he stuffed the cheese chunk into his mouth he grabbed her wrist—hard—and wrenched the knife free. With a brutal shove that sent her tumbling, he fled the byre. She scrambled to her feet and ran after him.

He was going for the horses! She had no idea his lurching gait could carry him so fast. Already he was inside the livestock byre and the horses were thudding about and whinnying with fear. The cow bellowed in dismay. Without hesitating at the door, Asa plunged through and leaped onto Jorgen's back. Her head brushed the shaggy turf ceiling as she pounded his shoulders with her fists. The assault sent him staggering. For a few dizzying steps she thought they were both going to topple but he managed to regain his balance. Grunting like a diseased animal, he swayed left then jerked right. She felt her grip loosen. Grabbing the woven neck of his tunic, she kept up her pummeling even as she slipped. He repeated the move, jerking even harder and this time she fell, slamming into the ground with a breath-choking thud. Pain bored through her skull; her head exploded in a blinding display of flashing lights.

She couldn't breathe. She couldn't breathe at all! Her mind scrambled through its haze, trying vainly to put order to things while her chest was caving in, flatter and flatter, emptied of air. The blackness began engulfing her and she went slipping and spinning deep within herself. From that echoing distance she was somehow aware of hooves smashing the dirt just inches from her head before lifting away. And horse sweat—the thick, sour kind that comes from sudden panic—filled her nostrils. Then Rune's scream pierced the gloom. She knew it was Rune, not one of the other horses, and his distress brought her charging back to consciousness.

She sucked in a great gulp of air and dug her fingers into the dirt. She blinked, breathed, and pushed herself up in time to see a dark gash rip Rune's tawny neck. His eyes rolled to white. Trying vainly to scramble backward, he was losing his balance—and the knife came arcing down again, fast and true, like a wicked bolt of lightning.

Not even fully conscious yet, she targeted the skald. She drove off the dirt and rammed him at the knees. He buckled like a stand of barley beneath the scythe. The two of them fell together in a chaotic heap of tangled boots, elbows, and flailing fists. The horses careered around them, snorting and squealing. One of them leaped right over them as they tumbled.

Asa loosed all her fury; she scratched his greasy, pitted face and battered his chest and slammed a fist into his ragged teeth. Blood darkened his beard. He tried to block her blows, but they fell as relentlessly as hail. When he finally managed to catch her forearm and stop it midair, he gave it a vicious twist downward, roughly yanking her off him. The move tore a fire-hot pain through her shoulder and a cry from her lips. The cry hardened into a scream of determination, and the skald got only as far as his knees before she knocked him flat again. This time his chin hit the dirt at an awkward angle, and she saw the shock in his eyes as his arm flopped uselessly and the knife came free.

She buried one knee between his lumpy shoulders and braced the other against the ground. Both of them eyed the knife; its handle lay tantalizingly close. The skald wriggled beneath her.

He stretched his arm longer and longer, using his fingers to pull himself through the dirt. It took all her strength to keep him pinned while trying to reach over and past him.

She was almost there. He squirmed with surprising strength, and his middle finger scraped the handle. Alarmed, she made a desperate lunge. That teetered her off balance, and he seized the opportunity to heave himself upward and toss her off.

His fingers closed around the knife's handle. He was breathing hard, and for a moment she thought he was going to lie there, but with a rasping snarl he turned on her. His arm drew back and—as if she were watching it happen to someone else—she saw the point of the knife come stabbing through the air straight at her.

Instinct jerked her aside, and the knife seemed to bury its blade in her tangled hair, though another fire seared her neck. He lifted the knife again. She rolled to safety, calling for Rune.

She couldn't see him but she knew he'd come. And just as she pulled an arm across her face, her world became a storm of stamping hooves and sickening thuds. There was another scream—a man's scream this time—and she found her feet and stumbled away. From the other side of the byre she watched in queasy horror as the dun horse savaged the skald. He reared all the way to the ceiling and brought his sharp hooves down on the cowering man. Jorgen hugged the wall but Rune turned and delivered a barrage of kicks. The skald managed to twist out of the way and take a few running steps, but Rune chased after him, his teeth clacking like iron on iron. He trapped the skald in the corner.

Jorgen turned to face the furious animal. Panting, and cradling his ribs, he yet managed to lift the knife high and charge at Rune. The knife slashed across the horse's chest.

Every pore of Asa's skin felt Rune's pain, and she screamed with him. To her bewilderment, Rune didn't retreat. He lifted onto his hind legs again, an effort that spattered blood across the skald's face and arms. The hoof that glanced off the man's shoulder crumpled him, but as he fell Jorgen kept stabbing the knife at the horse's legs.

She had to get Rune out of here; the horse was going to kill himself trying to protect her. She ran up the earthen ramp to push the byre door all the way open. The red stallion nearly knocked her down rushing through it; the bay followed on his heels.

"Rune!" He flicked an ear but reared up again, striking relentlessly at the skald. She'd never seen him in such a rage. "Rune! Here!" He turned his head then, giving the skald a free opportunity to deliver the death blow. "Here!" she yelled at the top of her voice, and the horse lunged toward her as the knife swept the empty air. She raced ahead of him through the doorway and darted aside, crouching slightly. The moment he shot through, she leaped for his mane and pulled herself across his back. Barely holding on, she urged him toward the black shore.

The skald's anguished howl echoed in their wake.

ÁTTA

If not for the giant silver brooch of a moon pinned against the night sky, they might have tumbled over rocks or tangled themselves in the ocean's debris. But with it they were able to mark the shoreline by its undulating ribbon of moonlit waves.

Was it just yesterday they'd galloped here? It was too much to ask of an old horse, especially after Jorgen's attack, so when they were safely around the first finger of land and alone with the sea, Asa tried to coax Rune to a walk. Clutching his thick mane, she thrust her heels forward and fought the pounding momentum. "Whoa." That got her nothing but jounced off balance, and for a few dizzying heartbeats the ground rushed perilously close. "Whoa!" she hollered again as her knee sought a grip. She managed to right herself, but Rune kept charging along the shore, carrying her with him. The gray-whiskered prankster was taking full advantage of galloping bridle-less!

Again she tugged on his mane, nearly yanking the hairs from their roots, and this time she stretched her leg all the way to the point of his shoulder and thumped hard. "Whoa!" she demanded. Rune sank to a halt. His immediate and indignant snort, though, which he trumpeted through the dark, denied his submission. He pranced sideways, swished his tail, and shook his head in defiance. He could go on, he seemed to claim, even with his breath coming in roaring gusts like the waves at his feet.

Feet that were limping. Now that fear no longer buoyed their flight, she detected the unevenness in his gait and hastily slid off him.

Blood splattered his shoulder and forelegs and oozed, glistening, from two gashes along his neck and a deeper one under his chest. Cupping a hand beneath his jaw, she coaxed him to take a few steps. His wincing effort showed it was the chest wound that hurt the most. But he wasn't trembling, wasn't dropping to the ground and giving up. This was Rune, after all. Between his labored breaths, he managed a soft nicker, a depositing of his trust in her.

She needed something with the healing color of black—a raven's feather or a polished stone or . . . even a simple black thread. *That* she had in her tunic. Admittedly it was more of a woody brown, but in the moonlight the piece of wool she was working free of its woven pattern would serve as black. She picked the thread loose, in and out, in and out, until she could snap off a length with her teeth.

"Bone to blood," she chanted as she tied the thread around Rune's foreleg, as close to the chest wound as she could get. "Blood to sinew and flesh to hide. Odin, I call to you! Heal!" Rune worked his lips across the top of her head as she repeated the chant a second and third time. Already the deepest wound seemed to be dripping less. Satisfied, she rose.

What were they going to do now? Where were they going to go? She looked up and down the strip of shoreline, and for the first time she became aware of the stinging pain in her neck. Running a hand behind her ear, she felt a stickiness that could only be blood—*her* blood. She'd narrowly avoided being killed herself. With a renewed sense of danger, she looked behind to make sure Jorgen wasn't following.

The frosted light of moon and stars revealed no shadows slipping along the path leading from the fjord. They were alone. Safe for now. But where were they going to pass the remainder of the night? Such exhaustion gnawed at her bones that she felt she could very nearly make a bed atop the shore's mosaic of rocks. As she stroked Rune's face a blast of sea spray reminded her they needed to find some place more sheltered. Hating to push him on, she nonetheless whistled her command, and they turned away from the familiarity of their fjord and began walking. The unnatural sequence of crunching steps punctured by a sudden grunt and thud marked Rune's hobbling progress. Each snort of pain stung her afresh.

The sheer cliffs on their right offered no shelter whatsoever. When the two followed the shoreline inland, poking along the base of the ridged fingers, the steep forests loomed so dark and forbidding that they stuck to the narrow strip between mountain and water rather than risk their lives on those precipitous black slopes. The moon lit their way for a while, but when it finally slipped behind the mountains, taking its icy light with it, the boundary between water and land bled into shadow, and Asa, at least, walked blindly. For comfort she slipped her hand through the coarse fringe of Rune's mane, resting it lightly on the warm crest of his neck. He was moving more steadily now, and though she had to hunch her stiffening shoulders against the frigid gusts hurled from the ocean, they went on searching for shelter without mishap.

It was when they were trudging around a shadowed cove lying deep between two craggy, rock-strewn knuckles that an eerie whine sounded above them. Rune stopped, ears pricked toward the darkness. Was something stalking them? Had Jorgen somehow gotten ahead of them? She listened harder. Only the innocent splashing of water against the rocky shore broke the silence. But as she hesitated, frozen in place, she realized the damp cold was seeping through her clothing. She envisioned her mother curled beneath the sheepskins and feather quilt. If she hurried, if she turned around right now, she could be back in the longhouse lying beside her mother before she awoke.

But Jorgen would be there too.

Rune's sudden snort and shy from underneath her hand shot her through with alarm. He stood tensed, ready for flight. What? What was out there? As hard as she tried, she couldn't see anything. Yet every nerve in her own body screamed at her to go back.

No. She couldn't—she *wouldn't*—risk Rune's life by returning to their clan. They'd have to sacrifice her first, because if they killed her horse, well . . . Odin himself would have nothing on her fury. Though her heart drummed in her ears, she disguised her fear with murmurs of soothing nonsense and sidled over to Rune. She scratched his withers and, after a few more snorts followed by another long stretch of silence, he relaxed.

Side by side they continued, finding nothing more dangerous than additional dark shore stretching ahead. Like the walking dead they plodded, step after numb step, mindlessly retracing yesterday's gallop—or was it the day before that the *Sea Dragon* had sailed? She shook her head. When was the last time she'd slept? Her mind tried to sort the events, but images of Jorgen leered through the haze. His hungry, heavy-lidded stare. The pale brown mole at his temple. The cheese crumbling in his hand.

He wanted to be clan leader, she knew that much now. Which, she realized with the sudden clarity of a light beaming through a cracked door, was completely different from wanting to lead the clan. Jorgen wanted the power that came with being first, of being on top. He coveted the seat of honor. But leading the clan meant putting everyone else's needs ahead of your own. That's what her father had done. His trip into the storm was foolhardy in so many ways, but he'd done it for the good of the clan. *He* was a true leader.

If he never . . . No, she wouldn't think of that. She wouldn't think of anything except keeping herself and Rune alive.

And the other horses? It seemed her mind had to gallop

through all the dire possibilities. Well, they'd fled the byre. She didn't know what they'd find to eat, but hopefully Jorgen's knife wouldn't find them. Her mother had said to keep the horses safe, and so far they were.

The stars spun above them, following their own dark course, and still no path climbed into the shelter of the forest, no rocky niche offered refuge on the shore. The night's cold rimed her cheeks, pulling the skin taut; the ocean's breath dripped from her nose. When she blinked, droplets quivered on her lashes.

Apparently the months of watered soup and bitter bread had carved a hollow inside her. She didn't realize how weak she'd become, though, until she was slipping behind Rune's shoulder and then his flank, and finally she was trailing him. Nor did she notice the ocean's rising tide creeping ever closer to them. Unheeded, it swallowed so much ground that when they reached the tip of the middle finger of land, the snub-nosed bluff there loomed straight out of the oily black sea. There was no dry passage around it. She couldn't judge the water's depth and stood peering into the darkness, listening to the waves rush up, splash against the walls, slap down, and recede. Rush, splash, slap, and recede. Rush, splash, slap, and recede. The dreamy recitation held her entranced, unmoving.

Rune banged his head against her. Getting no response, he nudged her again, harder. Finally he nickered his concern, four honeyed notes that started deep and descended deeper, reaching through her numbed darkness. Asa grabbed hold of them with the desperation of a drowning person and let them lift her up and onto his back.

Rune plunged ahead with enough confidence for both of them, although the icy waves leaped up to soak his belly and she had to lift her feet to his withers and ride hunched, swaying, like a bird on a windblown bough. Because of him they managed to round the bluff without being washed away. They returned to the ever-narrowing strip of crunching sand and proceeded.

After a longer period, when the fog lifted from her mind again, she whispered to him to halt and slid off. Gently she touched her fingers to each dark slash. The neck wounds felt sticky; the bleeding had stopped. His chest wound still oozed blood but much more slowly now. The dark wool thread still wrapped his leg. Holding two fingers to it, she repeated her chant to Odin, demanding him to heal her horse. Then, shoulder to shoulder, they took up walking again.

She had no idea how deep the night was or when the sun would appear, *if* it would appear for them. Inside her shoes her feet felt as if they had hardened to ice, and each crunching step seemed to shatter the bones, shooting stinging pangs up through her legs. The water-laden air left a briny moisture in her lungs that further weighed her down. In her stupor each step seemed to be carrying her from this world into the next. She didn't really care anymore. Rune was faring no better: His head drooped past his knees, and his hooves dragged wet furrows across the sand.

At last they reached the steep-sided cliffs banding the

shadowy fjord beyond the fourth finger and couldn't go any farther. As black as the shore was, as dark as the vast sky was, the fjord was blacker. Silent. A bottomless cauldron that swallowed light and sound. The end of the world. She could see nothing, and standing there, frozen to the bone and with no place to keep walking toward, she gave in. Her journey was over.

Looming over them like a giant cresting wave was a bluff much taller than the previous one. Wind had carved a slight hollow at its base and, more recently, knocked a massive chunk of stone onto the shore. The narrow space behind the fallen rock wasn't much of a shelter, but it was high enough to be out of the tide's reach. They could squeeze in there and be partly protected from the wind. They could fend off the cold's hunger a little longer.

At her urging, Rune followed her step by halting step beneath the angled walls of the bluff. She had to duck her head to avoid the rough outcroppings, and she could hear the stone scraping his withers. When they'd wedged themselves behind the fallen rock, she turned, tugged on Rune's forelock, and pointed to the ground. It was a cue she'd taught him years ago, and obediently he folded his knees and dropped with a wheezy groan.

She dropped onto her own knees. Reaching through the darkness, fingering his coarse mane and fuzzy neck and iron shoulder, she again felt for and found each sticky wound. They'd not reopened, but some of Rune's spirit seemed to have run out with his blood. He seemed shrunken, bony. Heaving a sigh, he flopped his huge head across her lap and closed his eyes. Out of habit she stroked the hollows above them awhile, then buried her fingers in the warmth trapped beneath his thick mane.

All she could see between the rock in front of them and the bluff above was a horizontal strip of dark sky. Wispy clouds banded the view, but thousands of fiery embers from the gods' fires burned there too. Was her father staring at these same bits of light? Or had his eyes forever closed to their brilliance? How much longer would her own eyes be open? Judging by the ragged haze clouding her vision, not much longer. What would take her and Rune? Cold? Hunger? A knife? Toughening herself to live with the choice she'd made, and if necessary to die by it, she began rocking, waiting for whatever was coming.

IX
NÍU

Birds. Huge, rough-voiced birds, calling to her. Loudly. The geese! Drawing summer on their wings.

Asa struggled to waken, her heart already skipping. She would tell her mother first—nudge her shoulder and whisper the incredibly good news—and then they'd tell the rest of the clan, and together they would breathe in the promise of warmer days and greening grass and new life. They'd made it!

Except that when she pushed onto her elbow, it dug into damp sand and not her straw mattress. The fingers she lifted to her face rubbed stinging granules of the same stuff into her eyes. She bolted upright, blinking in pain. Where was she? Handicapped by her watery vision and the predawn gloom, she managed to identify a massive rocky wall an arm's length in front of her and she felt the pressure of its mate at her back: the shore's bluffs. She was waking near the ocean—and she wasn't alone. Within that same arm's length she saw booted feet poking from beneath a dark gray cloak. Her heart left off its skipping to drum an alarm; she craned her stiff neck upward, following the shrouded form. Silhouetted against a horizontal strip of sky that still sparkled with a few stars was the deeply furrowed and well-weathered face of a one-eyed old woman. Scowling. Behind the woman's shoulder a large black bird—a raven—strutted back and forth on the rock.

Asa had never given ravens much consideration, but at that moment this one seemed the very embodiment of evil. It was the bird's demanding, guttural calls that were shattering the morning. *Gronk. Gr-r-o-n-nk.*

She had to flee. Where was Rune?

Through the slits of her crusted eyes Asa spotted him beyond the rock, closer to the ocean. Only his uplifted head showed against the strip of sky, but she could tell he was annoyed, and then she saw why: Another raven swooped past his ears, worrying him with beak and claws and that same harsh cry. Rune shook his head as his teeth snapped on air.

The raven on the rock complained again, loud and insistent, which brought her back to her own tenuous situation. It was shifting anxiously from foot to foot and making hungry stabs with its beak. But not at her, she realized—at something cupped in the palm of the stranger. While she stared, thickly, trying to get her mind to work, the hand extended toward her; the palm opened. On it lay a nut-brown barley cake.

In a flash she had it inside her mouth, her tongue swelling with water, her eyes brimming with unexpected tears. A rich oily flavor permeated the cake; it tasted of the summer sun, nothing like her clan's recent crumbly cakes stretched too far by bark and peas. And like a flash of sunlight on a clouded day, it was gone too soon.

To her amazement, her shrunken stomach protested the thick sweet lump, and immediately vomited up the precious food. She flushed. What was wrong with her? And what would the old woman think of such ingratitude? Doubled over, breathing fast, she didn't dare look past her own knees.

Teetering on the edge of living, she watched with bewilderment as the woman calmly reached into the pouch slung across her shoulder. Another cake appeared and, ignoring the anguished rumblings in her stomach, Asa snatched it and devoured it in three barely restrained bites. It hurt but she held it down.

The raven, obviously jealous, shrieked and unfurled its wings as if they were weapons. The feathers slid apart with the sound of rustling leaves. Even without the sun, their blue-black color glinted to iridescence. When the bird opened its bill to repeat its displeasure, its stub of a black tongue twitched spasmodically. The woman elbowed the creature aside to offer a third cake, and this time Asa remembered to nod a thank-you. She shoved it into her mouth with no less haste, however, and as she was plucking the crumbs from her lap, she cast a curious, upward glance at the stranger.

The woman was old to be sure, older than any person Asa had ever seen, and the winters she carried seemed to have dragged her into a permanent stoop. That put her in the same no-neck posture as the raven at her shoulder, which wasn't the only feature they shared. Its downward-curving bill was mimicked in her drooping nose, the fleshy point suspended like a globule of cold sap. Its beard of feathers found a likeness in the blackberry-colored scarf she'd wound round and round to her chin. But while the bird continued to strut and fret, the woman stood motionless, her clawlike fingers gripping the pouch's leather strap with a strangulating possessiveness. Her good eye, which she fixed on Asa, was the palest of blues and nearly concealed by folds of gossamer wrinkles, though that did nothing to diminish its intimidation. Even the grotesque hollow beside it, empty of eyeball, seemed threatening. When an ocean gust whipped through the short white hairs not fastened into the woman's braid, it haloed them around her face in a display that was nearly majestic.

"Who are you?" Asa asked.

"Who are *you*?" came the reply. In her voice Asa found yet another resemblance to the raven: It, too, grated as harshly as splintering wood.

"Asa Coppermane."

A dismissive snort. "An unlikely enough name for a girl, though not a horse."

Rune, trying to escape the other raven's devilment, galloped up to the bluff and pushed his way into the narrow gap. His keen senses immediately detected the barley. Brazenly he bumped his muzzle against the pouch, demanding a share.

"Rune!" Asa scolded even as the woman was producing one of the precious cakes and feeding it to him from her palm.

"Ach! He's forgiven. The winters get longer and longer, and we old ones have to tend to each other." Her scowl belying her genial words—which made Asa wonder if it was a permanent expression—she pulled out yet another barley cake. Rune took it and, as he chewed, nodded his head with intense equine pleasure. The woman returned her attention to Asa. "I've heard of you."

"Of *me*? How? Where do you live?"

A storm cloud seemed to skid across the woman's face, screwing the scowl tighter. "You ask too many questions for one so young. Just how many winters have you seen?"

"Fourteen."

"Too few to ask so many questions. You should squawk less and listen more."

Asa found herself bristling. "My father is clan chieftain. He taught me to ask as many questions as I needed."

"How noble of him." The throaty response reverberated as from a deep chasm. "And how very nearsighted. He'd have better spent his time teaching you to divine some important answers, such as one for this question: What are you doing so far from your clan? You're a fool. I could have slit your throat while you slept and fed you to my birds." Sensing an invitation to a feast, the other raven flapped its way toward the rock and joined its twin in a raucous chorus—a crowd of two chanting for a sacrifice.

Flushed with new alarm, Asa climbed unsteadily to her feet. Every bone and sinew in her body ached. Her movements accidentally disturbed the hem of the woman's cloak, which released an odor of blood and something else strong-smelling but indefinable. "Thank you for the barley cakes," she said, pushing at Rune's chest to get him to back away. "I'll be off now."

With unnatural quickness, the woman had Asa's arm in her grip. "Off to where?" Beneath her angular brow her one birdlike eye glinted, callous and cold.

Ice chugged through Asa's veins. She'd thought it would end differently; she had expected hunger or a storm to take them, but it was going to be this stranger. This was how she was going to die.

The woman shook her arm. "Off to where?" she repeated.

"To my clan. They'll be wondering where I am."

That snort again. "Who will—the dead ones or the dying ones? Who will be wondering about a headstrong girl who took her horse and ran off in the night? Who will care?"

Jorgen will. That thought came to her unbidden, and while she knew it was true, the idea made her squirm. Instead she answered, "My mother will care."

The woman released her arm with a dramatic flourish, the fingers of her rheumatic hand splayed against the lightening sky. She sucked in a sharp breath as the fingers stiffened; her blue eye rolled upward and back until only the mucous, yellowy white showed beneath her fluttering lid. "Your mother is dead."

All the smells trapped in the close space conspired to strangle Asa: the moldy dampness lining the dark crevices; the sour haze enveloping unwashed bodies; the briny tang of decay that filmed every surface, hovering. As if from a distance, she heard Rune's hide scrape the jutting wall and her own breath rushing out of her nose.

"That's not true."

The woman melted back into the present. She fixed her eye,

returned to its faded blue, on Asa. "So now you think you have answers. Tell me, then, little girl of only fourteen winters: Where is your father?"

A challenging tone, and an archly confident one, as if she already knew the answer and—Asa forced herself not to shiver—as if it were the same one given for her mother. She refused to accept either. A lot of people had died, true, but not her father and not her mother. Her mother was strong, and in a month's time or less she'd be standing at the shore welcoming the *Sea Dragon*'s return.

Jerking her chin toward the ocean, that great gray-green monster that swelled and retreated like a breathing entity, she replied, "He's there, sailing south." She didn't know for certain that her father had sailed south, but the details seemed unimportant. "He and six men from our clan sailed yesterday . . . or maybe it was the day before . . . to find food. Last year's rains rotted most of our crops and all our meat's gone. This winter a lot of people got sick and some . . ." But the odd woman had already mentioned the dead and dying. How had she known? "Your people," Asa began hesitantly, cautious about asking yet another question. "Has someone from your clan seen the ship . . . or heard news from it?"

She half-expected to be struck across the face, so she was taken aback when the woman laughed, revealing a stubble of small brown teeth. "I don't have a clan, unless you count these two black beasties here." She indicated the ravens, which had turned to tormenting each other with knocking bills and indignant cackles.

"Then where do you live? How do you live?" Asa couldn't help it; she asked questions. She had *always* asked questions. They spilled out of her as naturally as breathing.

The woman ignored her to scold the two quarreling birds. She made a throaty noise, sort of a drawn-out croak ending in a clacking of her tongue. Her raven speak halted the birds' bickering. One lifted into the air and flapped to a perch on her left shoulder while the other hopped onto her right. They bobbed and conversed anew in a soft, whining language that blended human and bird. Reaching into her pouch, she fed each one something small, something different from the barley cakes. That got Rune's attention and he nickered. The woman handed him another barley cake, then flicked her fingers at him, sweeping him away. Obediently he backed out of the space and wandered off toward the shoreline. They both watched him in silence before the woman turned Asa's questions back on her. "Where are *you* going to live? *How* are you going to live?"

"I don't know." The answer, inadequate even to her own ears, tightened her jaw. "Last night our skald tried to kill him," she said, nodding toward Rune, "so we ran away. If we're going to stay alive we have to find food." To let the woman know she wasn't expecting any more handouts, she explained, "I'm going to search the shore some more, then I'm going to try to get up into the mountains, look for leeks or some fallen nuts. If there's a lake, I can catch a fish."

The woman blinked dispassionately. "A leek. A fish. Why not

a barley field? Why not a whale? You are thinking only of a single mouthful."

A whale. Her mouth leaped to water. How long had it been since she'd tasted boiled *gryn*, salted *spikihval*, chewy *mylja*? Two summers ago, at least, when that unbelievably enormous whale had stranded itself. She swallowed her saliva to her stomach's disappointment. Such thoughts were ridiculous, precious time wasted on extravagant dreaming. If she and Rune were going to stay alive, they had to begin searching out food for their very next meal, not go chasing after a feast for a season. "Well, two mouthfuls is what we're after right now," she said, pulling her cloak around her. She began making her way to Rune, newly realizing how stiff and sore she was. "Thank you for the barley cakes."

"You don't want a whale?"

That involuntary rush of water crossed Asa's tongue again. A pleading rumbled in her belly. Temptation sat on one hand, suspicion on the other. She paused, considering. If this strange woman knew of a stranded whale, she could ride back and tell her clan. A whale would feed them for months, well into the summer. A year from now the oil would still be lighting their lamps; the bones would be crafted into smoothing boards and gaming pieces and traded for other foodstuffs.

"Ach! I see it in your eyes." The ravens bobbed noisy agreement. "You want a whale." The stoop-shouldered woman extended a claw. "Then you will have to follow me."

X
TÍU

How she ached! Both Asa's shoulder and hip felt as bruised as bottom-of-the-barrel apples, and a raw knob on her knee protested every step. As she followed the old woman up the twisting path hidden among the spray-darkened boulders, her tongue kept seeking out the swollen ridge inside her lip, a tender spot that still tasted of blood. She paused to check on Rune, and in brushing the windblown hair from her eyes, she accidentally bumped her nose. The unexpected sting brought a gasp.

What was Jorgen's condition, then? With a flash of heat she hoped he'd suffered more. She envisioned him awakening to debilitating pain—how would he explain it to the others?—and imagined him fingering the scratches she must have left on his face. That rekindled the memory of his greasy skin beneath her nails, and her stomach upended. Hastily she wiped her hands on the nearest boulder. Not enough. Scooping up some coarse earth, she scrubbed both hands until a raw, tingling sensation replaced the greasy one. There. Now if she could only so easily scrub herself free of the man.

But things were going to change. She and Rune were off to find a whale. There would be enough food to bring everyone back to health. Jorgen would be forced to pack up his awful stories and slink away from her father's empty seat. And the rest of them would manage to survive until both summer and the men returned.

Assuming there *was* a whale, that is. A nagging doubt girdled her belly like a tightening rope. She was putting an awful lot of trust in a stranger, and a peculiar stranger at that.

Just look. The old woman could have been one of her feathered companions, the way she bent forward at the hip, climbing in a stiff, birdlike walk. An occasional bobble brought her elbows up for balance, and the cloak trailing over them resembled wings, but she never used a hand to steady herself.

The ravens, meanwhile, circled above, rising on the updrafts until they were only black dots against the pearly morning sky. There they initiated their own game. First one bird would fold its wings and plummet, spinning, rolling, and tumbling, until lifting itself out of the dive at the last moment with an exuberant call. Accepting the challenge, the other bird would then fold its wings and plummet, mimicking the same spinning, tumbling combination, but adding some unique flourish. The intricate dives were repeated again and again, and the ravens' unfettered spirits lifted her heart. She took that as further sign that things were changing for the good.

Around the next boulder the path shot steeply upward,

hugging the cliff wall so closely as to be little more than a chalky band of sunlight. There wasn't room for a horse, and just as that thought came to her she heard the sudden clatter of rocks and pebbles, a surprised grunt, and the sickening sound of scrambling hooves. She spun, her heart exploding.

Rune had managed to stop his fall but he balanced precariously, one back leg wedged between two rocks below the path, the other folded at a high, awkward angle, grasping for solid ground. Gathering himself, he made a desperate lunge. More pebbles skidded down the embankment, but he remained captive. His anxious whinny tore through her.

In an instant she was back to him, a hand on his sweating neck. Blood reddened the ankle of his trapped leg. "Whoa, whoa," she soothed, forcing the fear from her voice while her mind raced. How was she going to pull him free? And even then, how was she going to get him turned around and safely down to the shore? The path was so dangerously narrow, the cliff way too steep. Glancing up, she met the woman's impatient scowl.

"He can't do it," Asa called.

That brought the one-eyed stranger picking her way back down the path. Tugging Asa aside with an unnatural strength, she forcibly seated her on a boulder. "Flap will help," she said, and thrust out her arm. Immediately one of the ravens came spiraling through the air. A whoosh of cold swept Asa's face as it landed. The big black bird neatly folded its wings before sidestepping to the woman's shoulder and bobbing in anticipation. With one gnarled finger she ruffled its chest feathers until it fell completely still. Then she lifted her lips close to its face. As she murmured, it cocked its head, and its shiny brown eyes rolled and blinked. Asa couldn't make out words; it appeared to be more raven speak, because as soon as the woman was finished the bird gave an agreeable *kr-r-up*, spread its wings, and lifted upward with a heavy flapping. It circled once, then swooped close to Rune's ears and soared ahead. Encouraged, Rune struggled. That sent a few more rocks tumbling into the chasm, and he gave up.

Asa started for him. "He can't—," she began, but the woman had Asa's arm in a twisting grip that choked the words from her.

The raven returned. It circled again, its black wings spread nearly as long as Asa was tall. Then, voicing a harsh *kra*, it dived toward Rune's back. The attack by beak and claw startled Rune into a leap forward and sent more rocks skittering. A second attack propelled him to scramble a few more steps and he regained the path, breathing heavily. But the raven wasn't finished. It kept up its barrage until it had driven Rune past the two women—they sucked themselves tight to the cliff wall—and on up the trail.

The old woman grinned smugly. "He *can*." She released Asa's arm and continued up the path. Asa had no choice but to follow, bewildered.

Before long they were well into the shadowy fjord and beyond the reaches of daylight. Higher and higher they climbed, farther and farther away from the shoreline and any possibility of a stranded whale, and her doubt grew suffocating. Why did she continue to follow? They were obviously going in the wrong direction. Was she really so spineless?

"Mylja."

The word came drifting down the trail without the woman even turning around, and the hairs on the back of Asa's neck stirred. How did the woman know? Just how did she know she could lead Asa on to the edge of the world by dangling the promise of her favorite meal: melted whale blubber spread thickly across a chunk of warm flatbread? It was a treat she'd enjoyed only that one lovely summer, but one that she'd often mused of since, especially when sitting beside the fire mouthing its crumbly, barren substitute.

"*Mylja.*" The word floated past her again, whispered this time. Or arising from the fog inside her own mind. Was she losing her wits? Under some sort of spell? She needed to stay alert; this was unknown territory—not just the path, but the woman, too. Her heart thumped spasmodically as she recalled her father's oft-repeated warning: The cloak of a stranger hides helping hand . . . or deathly dagger.

Why hadn't she brought Astrid's knife with her? She had no way of defending herself if the woman attacked. One quick shove would send her plummeting to the jagged rocks below. Her scream would be swallowed by the ocean's frigid waters. No one would ever know, she thought with a twinge, and before long, no one would even remember her. Determined to avoid such a humiliating fate, she gingerly wiped the mist from her face and pulled her cloak about her more tightly.

For what must have been half the day they skirted the fjord, though who could sift morning from night while traveling within the ever-present dusk hemming the towering cliffs? Asa found that the fjord wasn't that long, though it was unusually narrow. The ocean breezes had died at the shore, leaving the chasm eerily still. Far, far below, iron-black water noiselessly lipped toothlike boulders. A sense of otherworldliness, of stepping through a dream, enveloped her. She wished Rune weren't so far ahead. He was her safety, her means of quick escape. Having the old woman positioned between her and her horse only added to her unease.

Time dragged on and Asa's steadily throbbing head measured its passage. When she thought she couldn't possibly take another step without shattering into fragments, she found herself on the opposite side of the fjord at the camouflaged entrance to a cave. A rack of drying fish leaned there, protected from the mist by an overhang. The old woman squawked. Muttering a spate of grunts and cackles that again blended human with bird, she hastily dragged the rack inside. There she carefully inspected each silvery fish with a probing finger. Asa couldn't help but notice that the eyes on every fish had been neatly gouged out. The blind victims hung by their tails, mouths rigidly agape.

As she waited outside with Rune she also noticed a trail of white bird feces splattering the cliff wall. She followed it upward to an enormous raven's nest, the largest she'd ever seen. It was built directly above the cave's entrance, protected by its own rocky overhang. Thousands upon thousands of broken twigs and small branches had been intricately woven together over what must have been many summers. The two ravens already perched on its jagged rim, hurling their cries at Rune and Asa, and for the first time it occurred to her that the birds were a mated pair.

Apparently satisfied with the state of the drying fish, though her frozen scowl suggested otherwise, the woman beckoned. Asa hesitated—she'd been promised a whale, and there was certainly no whale here—until an unexpected gust of cold rain chased both her and Rune into the woman's home. The ravens yelled their distress.

Smoke filmed the cave. Its odor blended with the musky-sweet fragrance of rotting food and the faded stench of blood. The high-ceilinged room was quite dry, though, and surprisingly welcoming considering the mess: In a word, the woman's home was *havoc*—complete, day-after-the-storm havoc.

How many winters had passed, Asa wondered, since the floor had met with the cleansing bite of a broom—if it ever had? Animal bones of all sizes littered it, tangling with clumps of cobwebby feathers and shreds of hide and fur. Piled baskets teetered haphazardly among ancient wooden barrels, many lying on their sides. Some spilled moldy fishing nets; others dribbled grain or the twisted roots of vegetables. Bundles of dead pine branches sagged in one corner, their thinning brown needles silently cascading downward. And poking from the gloom at the rear of the cave were several splendid sets of antlers. But Asa also saw art amid the disorder. Large stones of various and unusual colors had been placed about the room in careful arrangements: two mottled ones here, three strangely smooth red ones on a ledge over there. Odd.

Posts and beams had been erected to support makeshift rafters, and from these rafters hung a year's bounty of both smoked and dried meats: the entire haunch of an elk, strips of smaller animals, netted chunks of green-tinged mutton. Her newly expanded stomach rumbled. So much food. Would the woman share it? Could she take some back to her clan? But where was the whale?

She noticed Rune nosing through the pine branches. His inquisitive snorts were scattering the fallen needles, and she moved closer to make sure he didn't get into something he shouldn't.

"Now," the woman said, "I'll boil some water for tea—give chase to the chill."

Asa nodded. She wiped her dripping nose and watched as the woman, with some effort, lowered herself beside the ringed hearth. It took a very brief time for her to coax a fire from the ashes. After lacing branches across the flames and swinging the iron pot into place, she rose and began pawing through some bowls on a nearby shelf, making turbulent rustling sounds.

"Do you prefer nettle or mint? I'm not accustomed to visitors so I don't have a royal selection." Glancing over her shoulder with the one-eyed scowl that was beginning to grate on Asa, she answered her own question. "No, you're but a child. A child wants something sweet. I've a bit of dried apple around here somewhere . . ." Her voice eroded into that strange, soft cackling and cooing as she rummaged through other bowls, peering close with her one good eye.

Asa's teeth clenched. She was a guest here, but this was the second time today she'd been called a child and she was having no more of it. She was fourteen, a chieftain's daughter—certainly no child. Only good manners—and prodding hunger—held her to her place. The moment she learned the whereabouts of the stranded whale, however, she and Rune were abandoning the old woman to her bird-rabid ramblings.

The water reached a boil and a handful of dried apple slices were dropped into the pot along with some apple leaves crumbling on their twigs. Soon they were seated next to the fire's warmth, cupping steaming bowls in their hands. The woman had failed to offer her the guest's traditional seat of honor, yet another affront, so Asa sat cross-legged at her right, chin lifted in smoldering indignation. Rune sidled over to stand behind her. His nose rested lightly on her shoulder, the weight growing noticeably heavier as his eyelids drooped.

Although she didn't begin a conversation—as a polite host should have done—the woman apparently had words rolling around in her mind. Again and again she shifted positions, heaving a nasally sigh each time, but a foot would wiggle restlessly and she'd have to re-contort herself, and then a knee bounced or her other foot burst into movement. Asa tried to ignore her but, as if guided by their own will, her eyes kept stealing toward the unnatural hollow beneath the woman's bony brow. She'd never considered the space an eyeball possessed, but the indentation there was substantial, easily the size of a baby's fist. The smooth lid had been pulled shut and sewn in place with stitches only slightly more yellow than its own stubby white lashes.

Growing restless herself, she finally voiced the question that had been on her lips all day. "Is the whale somewhere near here?"

"What whale?"

That knocked a hole in Asa's belly. She set down her tea, inadvertently awakening Rune. "You said if I wanted a whale I should follow you."

The woman's shoulders jerked convulsively. Was she laughing—actually *laughing*? "I did say that," she admitted in a muffled attempt to choke back her amusement. "But I didn't say I *had* a whale. Where would I keep a whale here?" She indicated the darkened space around them and folded herself tighter, as if trying to smother her ill-timed humor.

Maddened, Asa climbed to her feet. "Then Rune and I will have to keep looking. Now."

"You'd never find your way."

The certainty of the words brought her up short. All of a sudden she felt trapped, moments away from being torn to bits like the other animals whose remains lay scattered about. She wanted to reach over and slap the leathery old face. And, breathing faster, she realized she wanted to slap herself, too, for being so stupid as to follow a stranger right into her lair. What would her father have said?

She eyed the distance to the cave's mouth, wondering if both she and Rune could get out alive. A sharp flapping announced the two ravens' approach. They came strutting into the cave, shaking the rain from their glistening blue-black feathers and turning their heads from side to side with imperious self-assurance. Rune pinned his ears.

She had to act. "*Is* there a whale?" she demanded.

"Of course. The sea is full of whales."

"Yes, but is there a stranded whale near here?" Such desperation in her voice.

"Not yet." The woman gazed up at her, sitting very erect and quite still now. "Though there will be."

Asa's frustrations boiled over. "You said if I wanted a whale I should follow you. You lied to me! Why did you lie?"

The two ravens shrieked and lifted up to flap about the room. A vase of milk-colored glass crashed to the floor, shattering. Something else plummeted from the rafters, landing with a double slap. Fur and feathers and bits of dried leaves swirled in a frenzy. One of the birds dived toward Rune's head and he had to duck to avoid being pecked.

"Quiet!" The woman's harsh cry brought the room to silence. With arthritic effort she rose first to her knees and then to her feet, and kept unfolding and rising until she appeared a full head taller than she previously had. In the firelight her one eye stormed a lightning blue. Obediently the ravens landed side by side on an overhead beam. They touched bills, then huddled together and watched with keen interest. "I don't need to explain myself to you," the woman said in hoarse but measured tones. "*I* am not a child."

Asa stamped her foot. "I am not a child either!"

The judgmental eye marked the gesture. "Then why are you running away? Why did you leave your clan under the thrall of that besotted skald Jorgen the Younger? What sort of chieftain's son—or daughter—abandons such responsibility?"

Had she mentioned the skald's name? How did the woman know it? Brushing aside the niggling questions, Asa answered emphatically, "I left to search for food."

"You ran away."

She hadn't. "I was protecting the horses. That was my father's wish, and my mother's."

"You stole what you wouldn't sacrifice."

Rodentlike scurryings of guilt poked Asa's insides. But they were accompanied by an ice-cold wariness of her host's intentions. "No one's going to kill Rune."

"Even if such a sacrifice would please the gods and hurry summer? Even if such a sacrifice would protect your clan?"

"What sort of a god wants a horse killed?" She burned. The tea seemed to have set her ablaze. She felt its liquid warmth pumping through her chest, caressing her ribs and strengthening her arms. The tips of her fingers stung with unseen bees.

"What sort indeed?" The woman kicked aside a basket to clear a path to a large, intricately carved wooden trunk. "Those that fancy themselves gods, I imagine." She lifted off a branch dangling dried berries, carefully set it on the floor, and opened the lid. Pawing deeper and deeper through its contents, she said, "Your clan, what's left of it anyway, is in danger—imminent danger. You know that."

Was it a question? Asa began stumbling over a response but was interrupted as the woman straightened, her arms full of fabric.

"Tell me, what would you do to rescue them?"

"Anything, of course, anything at all."

"Would you give up an eye?"

Horrific images flooded her mind. She became acutely aware of the warm liquid bathing her eyes, heard the lids blink, squishing, felt the balls swivel toward the cave's mouth again. Her own breathing roared in her ears. Taking a step closer to Rune, she said, "If my clan is in danger, I have to go back now."

The old woman looked at her ravens, who both bobbed excitedly, and then at Asa. "You will go back, but not today, and not until it's time. And when you do, you'll wear this." She shook out a beautiful woolen cloak dyed the deepest of blues. The firelight danced across the sparkling hem, embroidered with blue glass beads and clear crystal ones.

Asa's mind tumbled. She'd never seen the cloak before, and yet it was eerily familiar.

"It won't cost *you* an eye," the woman said, fastening the heavy garment around Asa's shoulders, "but rescuing your clan may demand something equally dear."

Stepping back, she thrust out both arms and a raven immediately alit on each one. She whispered to one bird and then the other, turned toward the cave's mouth, and gave a mewling cry that rose to a fierce screech. In unison the birds flapped off into the misty gloom.

Asa couldn't move.

XI
ELLIFU

Horses were fools, Jorgen thought. Given their freedom, they came sniffing back to the site of their winter imprisonment at day's end, creatures of dull habit, unable to think for themselves. Unable to imagine a life beyond their suffering.

He slipped away from the byre's wide-open door. He couldn't see them yet; they lingered somewhere up the hillside, hidden from him. But he could hear their hooves squishing through the mud and snapping the occasional twig. They moved restlessly; they wanted to come back. And when they did, he'd welcome them.

The advancing cold was making him impatient, though. What was the noise she made, the one that made them lift their heads, whinny happily, and come galloping? He curled his tongue between his lips and tried sucking air. The shaky whistle was met with a long silence and then a distant—and distrusting—snort. He tried blowing air, fitting his tongue against his teeth in different ways to get the right sound. Still the horses didn't show. He folded his arms across his chest and felt the air rush past his nostrils. He knew they would eventually, whether he called or not.

Twilight now, that curious interval that was neither day nor night, when the world seemed to hold its breath. A slippery time, he'd always thought, when shadows played tricks on men's eyes and not everything was as it seemed. He looked down the darkening path that edged the fjord all the way to the ocean. A spattering of crescent-shaped impressions marked the mud, their edges curling up and spilling outward. All that was left of her.

A hard spasm fired his belly. It snaked earthward, molten. He succumbed to the sensation, lost himself in the throbbing ache for a few shallow breaths, then abruptly smothered it. Better that she was gone. She had proven herself ungrateful, and worse, unworthy of his attention. Hadn't he offered her everything: gifts carved by his own artful hands; stories chosen especially with her in mind, ones brimming with the wisdom of his father and his father before him? He shifted his weight remembering how she'd brazenly argued his stories' wisdom. Such insolence! And last night—last night he'd proffered the remaining, tastiest cheese from his personal cache of food (his tongue watered as another hunger took hold), and how had she repaid him? He lifted one hand to trace the crusted ridges on his cheek, the work of her bony fingers gouging his skin. The latent heat flared again, sweetly torturous, and subsided. He exhaled with force.

He'd had to invent a story of a bear. (Which showed how gullible the people were, for when was the last time a bear had been seen in these lands?) But these were strange times, he'd reminded them, and went on to describe how he'd awakened to find Asa sneaking away with her horse. How he'd followed her into the night, calling for her to return—"Think of your mother!" he'd cried—until he saw something large, something shadowy—it had to be a bear, the biggest bear he'd ever seen—swat her to the ground. He told how he'd scrambled through the forest after them both, slipping again and again in the mud—that accounted for the bruises—and pushing past the unyielding branches that raked his face so mercilessly. But she was gone. Just like that, he related in a voice full of pitched woe, she was gone, and her horse had run off too, or been killed, and the other horses with it. Such a tragedy.

It touched him then how the girl's mother hadn't protested when he settled himself into the chieftain's place. She'd looked up and smiled, dreamlike, contented. Wisely she realized the importance of having a man leading the clan, a man who could and would safeguard their future, who'd make certain that no one who proved his—or her—worth went hungry.

Right off he guaranteed his ability to provide for them by passing around a small sack of hazelnuts. He'd discovered the bounty on his way down from the mountains, he explained, when he'd finally given up looking for Asa. Only one had questioned him: Tora, that outspoken pig of a woman. "How could so many nuts last the winter lying on open ground?" she'd challenged. "No other creature had found them?" All the while stuffing them into her wide, lipless mouth. He'd masked his disgust—inwardly marking her unworthy—and replied that he didn't know. Perhaps the gods had led him there. The forest was very thick, he explained—had they not seen the scratches on his face?—and the place where he had found them was hidden from all but the keenest eye. The hazelnut bush was growing above a deep cleft between two rocks, no wider than this: He'd held up his forearms, touching at the elbows and spreading only two fingers' width at the wrist. The nuts had obviously fallen into the cleft many months ago and piled there unseen. The woman had frowned, but her chewing closed her mouth to further questions.

An evening wind hurried up the fjord. He sniffed. A change coming? He flared his nostrils and sniffed more deeply, testing the cold air on the moist roof of his throat. For as long as he could remember he'd been able to predict a change in the weather by the smells carried on the ocean winds. Tonight he detected a subtle difference in the salt-laden odors. Were they fair or foul? Of that he wasn't certain. He lifted his gaze to the few stars speckling the deepening sky. Islands of luminous white clouds floated beneath them, their flat bottoms still glowing pink. Neither night nor day.

Hearing a movement, he turned slowly. The two horses were standing at the crest of the hill, looking down at him, their ears pointed. He made the smacking sound again and slapped his thigh. "Come! Come!" One horse snorted and lifted his head; the other took a cautious step backward.

Before he could call again, the strangest noise disturbed the air. It was the voice of an animal, he was certain, though it sounded like a nut cracking apart. He looked up to see two ravens flapping steadily toward him.

Ravens! He hadn't seen a raven in months, and now here was a pair of them, so strongly reminiscent of the regal pair Odin sent forth daily to gather information from the world that it had to be a good sign. One of the black birds gurgled, whined, and uttered a stream of hammering *tok*s, all of which the other echoed. It seemed they were speaking a language, and for a fleeting instant he wondered if they were speaking to him, perhaps carrying a message from the god himself. His father had sworn such had happened to him at one time. But the birds flew on in a true line and disappeared.

Idly he wondered if there was a way to entice their return. He'd never eaten a raven, but roasted over a fire any bird had to taste better than dried pea soup. He had hardly finished that thought when the pair came winging back, low enough now that he could see their black toes tucked tightly to their feathers. They were still trading chatter: rapid, burbling sounds punctuated by an occasional *quork*. Apparently they were oblivious to his presence, though he imagined the nearer bird tipped an eye toward him as it flew over.

He watched them go, then shook himself back to the present. He needed to get the horses into the byre. What were a couple of birds high in the sky when two meaty animals stood almost within reach? Wetting his lips, he smacked them—once, twice—hating the way it reduced him to a little girl. "Come!" he ordered loudly.

Quork. Quork. Strangely enough, his order had brought the

ravens wheeling around. Their chatter united in harsh cries as the birds suddenly spiraled out of the air to attack the horses. He felt his mouth fall open. The horses squealed, spun, and galloped out of sight. He heard them thundering up the hillside, the birds shrieking in their wake. And then everything was silent.

The wind charged his back, punching its cold through to his bones. His stomach growled. Images of roasting meat had readied him for a feast, and now he was as empty-handed as ever. To Nifelhel with those odious birds! Here he'd thought they were signs of good fortune and he'd been rudely deceived; they were nothing more than meddlesome creatures deserving of a miserable fate. Glaring at the darkening skyline, he roughly adjusted the cloak across his shoulders and heaved a sigh of frustration. Well, he could allow himself a few more of the hazelnuts he'd held aside. He hungered greatly, though, for a chewy piece of meat—one dripping with fat.

Just as he was turning toward the byre, that wavering moment of twilight vanished and night began to descend rapidly. He thought about leaving the door open in case those stupid horses returned on their own, but then he'd risk losing the cow. In sudden anger he slammed his shoulder against the wood planks and shoved the door closed. Let the fool horses shiver. They'd be more appreciative come morning.

He stalked down the path toward the longhouse—oh, why had he used his bad shoulder, the one he'd wrenched last night?—and as he did, he became aware of the two black birds again, congealing from the dusk. He shook his fist as they neared. If only . . .

From the edge of his eye he caught something falling. It was followed closely by an identical object and the instant he realized it, a damp clod thumped his head and crumbled down the back of his neck. Another splatted in front of him. Even in the gloom he recognized it as the fragmented turd of a horse. The birds' raucous chatter sounded distinctly like laughter as they melted into the night. He clenched his fists, shook himself off, and walked on.

XII TÓLF

Rune pranced, his long black tail swishing around his ankles with the agitation of storm-tossed waves. He struck at the cave floor and shook his head. Even when he ceased his fretting to momentarily look in Asa's direction, the skin covering his bony withers twitched with a spasmodic life of its own.

The woman's echoing wail had had the opposite effect on Asa. Though her heart pounded, she held herself motionless. Something was happening. Part of her seemed to fly away with the two ravens, yet the heavy blue cloak pinned her in place, crushing her neck and overloading her shoulders with its suffocating weight. Her head throbbed.

Rune snorted an emphatic blast that ricocheted off the stone walls. She was aware that he'd swung his head around and that his eyes sought the cave's arching mouth, the path to escape. If not for his loyalty, she knew, he'd go galloping through it.

She should join him.

That sudden and clear resolve stirred her to life. As carefully as she could, cautious not to make a sound, she began worming her way out from under the cloak.

"No!" The woman spun and pointed a finger. "What are you doing?"

That stiffened her and, caught as she was, burdened her one shoulder with the entire weight of the cloak. *Why* hadn't she brought Astrid's knife?

The pointed finger had no sway over Rune, however, and the clatter of his restless hooves grew louder. Their staccato cadence suggested imminent flight, and Asa's heart leaped into rhythm. "I really should go back to my clan," she explained in a falsely calm voice. The lone eyeball didn't blink. "If they're in danger—"

"They are," the woman interrupted authoritatively, "but your time's not yet ripe." Lifting the cloak from Asa with surprising ease, she seemed to hug it to her chest a moment before folding it in half and laying it across the open trunk. "The way will soon be dark. And I promised you a whale, which I don't have—yet—but I do have, let's see . . ." She turned and scurried over to a dark barrel. Sweeping aside some leaf litter, she lifted the lid.

Asa sidled next to Rune, stealing a desperate glance through the cave's mouth. Across the fjord the zigzagging fissures and rocky outcroppings had already gone murky; silhouettes were steadily dissolving in the falling dusk. How would they find their way?

As if sensing her thoughts, Rune nickered. Instinctively, she put a hand on his neck to calm him, at the same time realizing it wasn't anxiety in his utterance but anticipation. Grain was being scooped from the barrel into a shallow basket, and the lush sound of cascading granules had hooked his ears.

"Barley," the woman said, displaying the basket triumphantly.

Her approach elicited another resonant nicker from Rune, and when she set the basket at his feet he eagerly tore into the grain. The little mound, Asa thought, reddish yellow in the firelight, must seem as desirous to him as a pile of gold would to a man. And hard upon that thought came another: A well-fed horse could gallop that much faster and farther. "Thank you," she said, drawing herself tall. "He's not seen that much in a year."

In the woman's smile Asa was surprised to glimpse satisfaction, even a trace of motherly pride. The fan of wrinkles edging her one eye closely resembled her mother's, and the smile that made them pucker managed to soften her scowl as she prattled on. "Now for you, would you favor some klippfisk maybe? Or some fresh mussels? That's it! Mussels and leeks stewed in their own tempting broth. Something heartier than dried pea soup, eh? You'll stay the night now and share a meal." Whether it was an invitation or a command, she didn't wait for a response, but scuttled off to another barrel to plunge her bare arm deep inside.

Asa hadn't felt so spun about, so dizzy and disoriented, since her childhood days playing brigand and blindfold. Was this unpredictable old woman a danger or not? Rune had obviously lost his desire to flee now that he had his grain. He was nosing the basket across the floor with a colt's hunger, trying to snatch up every last kernel. She glanced outside. It *was* awfully dark. The night had blotted away all details that lay beyond the flickering shadows at the cave's mouth.

A shallow pot, dented and blackened with age, clanked as the woman pitched something into it. That was followed by another dull chink and clank, and then another. They were mussels, glistening blue-black mussels. She was pulling the dripping shells from the barrel, giving each a cursory examination, and rapidly filling the waiting pot. A noisy gurgle from Asa's stomach convinced her to stay. She was hungry, dizzy, and tired—oh, so tired. "All right," she agreed, unsure if that was even necessary. "What can I do to help?"

The woman shook droplets from her wet arm, darted over to another basket—moving now with the agility of someone much younger, a quite excited someone—and dug out a bulb of garlic, which she tossed to Asa. "Here, you can peel that," she said, and returned to the kettle.

In digging her fingernail beneath the flimsy, crackly skin, Asa punched a crescent into the garlic's flesh. Immediately she lifted the bulb to her nose and sucked in its fragrance. She loved the smell and taste of garlic—almost as much as her father did. For as long as she could remember he'd been teased for yanking young bulbs right out of the ground and crunching them between his teeth while he talked. The aroma within her cupped hands brought a pang; she could feel his breath warming the top of her head, sense his lips planting a kiss where so many had been planted over the years. Would she ever see him again, or had he and the others not survived the storm? And what about her mother? Rubbing her thumb across the bulb's waxy body, she recalled the knobs of bone strung along her mother's bowed neck. Had death always hovered so close to them?

She took her time tearing away the remainder of the garlic's loose-fitting skin, all the while watching the woman with curiosity. Just how much did this stranger know about her and her clan? The reference to dried pea soup could have been a guess—long winters usually waned with a few monotonous days of dried pea soup—but she spoke so confidently. Just how much did she know?

"You were wanting this, I suspect." With one brow arched enigmatically, the woman pushed a knife across the table, a knife so similar to Astrid's that Asa flinched with guilt. Flushing beneath the penetrating stare, she chopped the garlic as best as she could—the blade was somewhat dull—and slid the knife aside.

But she couldn't stop looking at it. Her palm ached to grasp the handle again, to hold the blade close to her, just for the comfort and protection pointed iron could provide. The old woman's back was turned. She'd never miss it in this mess, and almost before the thought was finished, Asa had secreted the knife in the waistband of her underskirt and was strewing the pile of garlic skins across the table and rearranging the jars and utensils to distract a questioning eye.

Once the garlic was tossed into the kettle, which was now nestled among the fire's embers, she was given the task of stirring the soup. She hunched over the pot, feeling the knife's cold iron poke her belly and wondering if the old woman knew. The mussels grudgingly parted their mouths as they cooked, surrendering the sweet flesh hidden inside, and her own mouth watered with anticipation.

Rune, having finished his grain, immediately walked a tight circle, swinging his nose across the cave floor. Three times he circled until, apparently satisfied, he buckled his knees and sank to the ground. His accompanying grunt expanded into a drawn-out sigh as his head drooped and his eyelids fluttered and closed. Asa smiled. He deserved a good rest.

It wasn't long before she and her host were seated beside the fire, cradling steaming bowls of mussel, leek, and garlic soup. Her stomach was growling so insistently that she bypassed her spoon to slurp some broth straight from the bowl, and it coursed through her with a nourishing heat. The muscles in her back relaxed—she hadn't realized how knotted they'd become—and her hips loosened. Guilt evaporated. She'd be joining Rune in no time, she thought with a silent chuckle. Hopefully without going face first into her soup. To her dining companion she said appreciatively, "This is good."

The woman only mumbled an unintelligible response, busy as she was with stabbing at a slippery mussel in her own bowl. She finally plucked up one blue-black disc with her fingers, critically eyed the partially opened shell, and flung it toward the cave's mouth. Asa expected its clatter to bring the two ravens' flapping descent, but the stone entry remained silent. Where had they flown off to?

The woman seemed to have no interest in her birds now; her focus was her meal. She held her head tilted so that her one eyeball looked straight down on the bowl, much like a gull targeting a surf-washed tidbit. After a few more stabbing motions she carefully lifted her spoon to her mouth, lips puckered eagerly. She sucked in the small lump of meat with a drawn-out burble and ignored the broth that trickled down her fuzzed chin. Then she tilted her head, aimed her spoon at another mussel, and returned to her stabbing.

The woman was truly odd, Asa thought, and as changeable as the weather: friendly and generous one moment, then aloof and temperamental the next. Well, she was here for the night, so she might as well make the best of it. "I still don't know your name," she said in a second effort to make conversation.

Engrossed in chasing a mussel around her bowl, the woman answered absently: "Wenda."

"And you don't have any clan?" Asa asked, searching the room once more for evidence of others.

The woman, Wenda, had her spoon with its glistening glob of mussel halfway to her seeking lips, but there she checked it to ponder the question. A moment passed; she shook her head and popped the mussel into her mouth.

Asa responded with the incredulity of a person who'd never lived a day unaccompanied. "Aren't you lonely?"

A wistful smile formed at the corners of Wenda's mouth as she chewed and gazed dreamily into the fire. Even after she'd swallowed and was resting her spoon inside her bowl, she kept staring glassy-eyed at the low flames, the smile fixed upon her face.

Had the old woman lost her way? Or was she purposely being secretive?

Behind her Asa heard Rune sigh with deep contentment and flop onto his side. She glanced over her shoulder to see him stretch his neck long and rub his cheek against the stone floor in short jabs, finding just the right spot. He heaved another sigh and went still.

At least her horse was untroubled. She, however, was becoming ever more vexed. Pursing her lips, she turned back and leveled a glare at the bemused old woman. Didn't Wenda care about being a good host? Why was her *guest* having to make all the conversation? It had been easier, she thought, to coax words from a feverish toddler.

As a nudge, she rattled her spoon inside her bowl. Nothing. She coughed, held her hand to her stomach, and coughed again, violently. The woman didn't so much as blink. Well, that was it; she was done trying. Then and there she vowed not to speak again unless spoken to, even if that meant passing the entire night in silence; lifting her bowl to her chin, she methodically sipped the yellowish broth with feigned concentration.

"I've not been lonely a single day of my life."

Asa peered across the bowl's rim to find Wenda smiling to herself with great pride.

"In fact, I can't even imagine being lonely," the woman went on. "I've loved and been loved, for a season at least. Now I have Flap and Fancy, and every day they bring me stories from the far corners of the world, the like of which you've never imagined. Through their eyes I've seen a people who can walk on water; I know of men who live in stone bee hives, as well as the immense distance to a land where the birds stand taller than children and yet not a one of them can fly." She began rocking forward and back in a pensive rhythm. "You may have two good eyes, child, but you'll never see these things."

The unexpected flood of words took Asa by surprise; the topic irritated like nettles. It was that talk again: of the two ravens acting like people, speaking like people. The talk of fools. She glanced toward the dark entry, but the two birds must have settled into their nest.

Wenda was awaiting her response, she sensed, but for a noticeably long stretch—while the fire crackled and spit, while the wind outside the cave paused to listen—Asa dragged her spoon through her bowl. What was she supposed to say? *How does a man walk on water? How can a raven tell you such a thing?* Well, she wasn't going to demean herself with such nonsensical talk.

Hunching her shoulders and keeping her gaze fixed firmly downward, she tried to wait out the awkwardness. But gradually, ever so gradually—and this, too, was odd—she began to feel Wenda's one blue eye boring through her. She felt it tapping on her skull at first, softly, insistently, demanding her to look up and then forcibly raising her chin by a will more powerful than her own . . . until she found herself staring directly into the hooded orb. Words in her mind swirled as if through a hailstorm. A question formed. No, she wasn't going to ask it. But the solemn gaze demanded that she ask, and although she tried to resist, although she tightened her jaw and felt the cords in her neck grow taut, she heard the words come spilling out of her mouth in a rush: "How did you lose your eye?"

There was a slight sense of satisfaction in the cave, an aura of success, before the retort was emphatically spat: "I didn't *lose* it." Wenda ratcheted her curving spine a *tomme* straighter. "Losing is an accident," she pronounced, "the result of brutality or coincidence. Losing requires no thought. I, however, gave a great deal of thought to the value of my eye and, after much thought, I decided to trade it."

Trade it! Willingly? Asa squirmed. She glanced toward the cave's mouth with new longing.

"I *thoughtfully* traded my eye for something that I hold more dearly than life itself."

The hiss of rain couldn't mask the insistent tapping Asa felt on her skull again: ask—ask! *What was more dear than life itself?* But this time she anchored her spoon in her bowl, pressed her lips together, and appeared fascinated with a green half-moon of leek floating in her broth.

"I've not had a moment's regret," Wenda said, speaking over the loudening rain. "You, with your child's fascination with appearances, may find me hideous, but I'm happy—mostly happy."

A deafening *whoosh* curtained the cave, thankfully drowning further conversation for the present. Wenda set down her bowl to snug her cloak tighter around her neck, and for the first time Asa noticed how thin the wrist was that extended from the sleeve of her tunic, how bluish the veins that webbed both hands. Was the woman ill? Maybe that explained the feverish talk. After all, she was incredibly old; who knew how many winters she'd seen? It was admirable, really, considering her age and frail health, how she held herself so erect. Even now she sat bolt upright, staring past Asa, waiting out the roar, her one eye blinking patiently.

The rain pounded and the wind blew, and when a handful of fat drops were hurled into the cave, Rune woke with a snort. As suddenly as the storm had started though, it exhaled and grew quiet. And as if she'd been merely waiting for that moment, Wenda directed her pale, one-eyed gaze upon Asa.

"Any more questions?"

She had more questions. Her head buzzed with them, in fact. Or maybe it buzzed with exhaustion. She watched Rune collapse full-out again. Firelight tipped the fur on his hipbone a pale gold and danced across his arching cage of ribs. Dried blood still matted his neck and chest; she'd have to attend to that come morning. From the shadows beyond him, the blue cloak shimmered faintly. *All right* . . . she indicated the cloak with a nod. "Where did that come from?"

Wenda picked at the fraying hem of her sleeve and, as if simply to aggravate her, replied, "Why do you ask?"

"Because I think I've seen it before." No, she hadn't really. "I mean, I heard a story told by our skald, Jorgen . . ." She was becoming ever more irritated with the woman's games. "But you must know of him, because you knew his name . . . ?"

The woman lifted her bowl to her lips, quenching her enigmatic smile, though she watched Asa steadily across its rim.

"Or I thought you mentioned him." Asa faltered. Her memories seemed to cloud. Why couldn't she think straight tonight? "But anyway, he told a story—I remember this much—about a woman who wore a blue cloak trimmed with crystals and glass beads. She was a seer, and"—she indicated the garment again—"that is exactly as I pictured it in my head."

The woman slowly sipped the broth from the bowl. She licked her thin lips then, deliberately and thoughtfully, and said, "Tell me about your skald. Has he served your clan well?"

The rotting odor of Jorgen's breath suddenly filmed Asa's face. The stench was as nauseatingly strong as if he knelt nose-to-nose with her at that very moment, proffering his yellow-toothed grin. She remembered how he'd eyed her father's empty seat, recalled how he'd edged his way around the fire toward it, pausing to share a word and thus disguise his true intentions, but all the while hungering for it as blatantly as a dog does the hunter's bloody prize. And of course there was that story he'd told the other day, the one meant to coax the clan into killing the horses. "No."

"No?"

"No," she repeated adamantly. Her insides twisted with a nagging discomfort: She shouldn't have galloped off and left her clan so vulnerable to his schemes.

"If your father was the clan's chieftain, as you've said, why didn't he act?"

"He didn't have a chance." She'd always defend him. "It was only after he sailed off with the other men that Jorgen tried to take control." Or was it? Something brought her father's frowning face to mind, a rare expression for his buoyant personality. His hands were clasped beneath his beard, his index finger stroking the crease of his lip. She knew he was bridling his anger. Oh, yes. It was the day they'd played the memory game, a stormy afternoon not so long ago. He'd suggested it as a way to pass the time, to take their minds off their grumbling stomachs and their whimpering children.

She remembered now. "I have a game of interest," he'd said with enthusiasm. A fierce, whistling wind sent straight from Odin mocked his small human voice, forcing him to repeat himself. "I have a game of interest," he said louder, and everyone looked up. "We shall imagine we are going *a-viking*, all of us, even the little ones." And at that, two of the younger boys had sat up from their mattresses. "I will name one item," he said, "that I will pack for our voyage, and then the person to my right will repeat that item and name an item that they wish to bring, and then the next person will repeat both items and add a third, and so on. Do you understand?" Heads nodded, some weakly but all willingly—all except Jorgen's. She remembered that also. For some reason she'd been watching him, over there in his corner whittling another of his spooky, bulbous-eyed creatures. He seemed to laugh to himself and shake his head derisively. He scratched his ribs, she remembered, and pointedly refused to join the circle forming around the fire.

"Good," her father had said, either oblivious to the skald's insolence or ignoring it. "Then I shall begin. On our seafaring voyage of good fortune, I shall bring a fearsome sword." He addressed Asa's mother, who was bent over a pair of breeches, needle in hand. "And you, dear?"

"I'll bring my fearsome needle," she said, "or this mending will never get done." A few of the women laughed at that.

"No, no, no. You have to repeat what I said—a fearsome sword—and then add yours."

"Oh, all right. I'll bring—"

"On our seafaring voyage of good fortune . . . ," he prompted.

Asa's mother sighed. "On our seafaring voyage of good fortune," she repeated, "I will bring a fearsome sword and three sharp needles."

"Good! And you?" Asa's father nodded toward Thorald.

"On our seafaring voyage of good fortune," Thorald recited, "I will bring a fearsome sword, three sharp needles, and a haunch of elk, well-browned and juicy." Laughter rippled around the room and the game picked up speed, some stumbling as the list grew longer and others helping complete the recollection. When it came to Jorgen's turn, he didn't even pause. Without error he rattled off the items named by the others, though pointedly omitting the opening phrase. Then he closed his mouth without adding his own article.

Her father, ever the peacekeeper, overlooked the defiance. "Well done," he said, and he meant it. "And what will you bring on our voyage?"

"Not a thing," Jorgen replied.

Her father sat taller. He watched the skald with new care. "And why is that?"

"Because I wouldn't join you on a voyage. Any boat you send out is bound for the bottom of the sea." He was referring to the fishing boat that had left ten days earlier and not returned. The two men on it, Olaf and Ari, were the clan's best fishermen, and they'd asked to take the boat out alone, not wanting to risk other lives. Asa's father had protested that the seas were too rough, the winter storms too unpredictable, but eventually he'd given in to the clan's mutinous mutterings that he was hoarding food for his precious horses while forbidding them to feed themselves.

"Olaf and Ari wanted to go," her father argued. "They were brave men who well understood the dangers."

"And now their wives have no one to feed them," Jorgen shot back. "Their children are left rudderless. As clan chieftain you should have stopped them."

All during this temperamental exchange the clan members

who'd swayed Asa's father with their grumblings held their mouths clamped shut to watch the spectacle with childlike interest.

"I was doing what the clan wanted," her father stated.

For the first time Asa recognized the backward logic in that, and it gave her a distinctly uneasy feeling, like balancing against an outgoing tide while the surf rocked your knees and the sand washed away between your toes.

"They don't know what they want," Jorgen had growled. He cast a black-eyed look upon the ring of blank faces. Then he turned his back to them all, bundled himself in his cloak, and squatted in his corner. What he did then wasn't known, though he muttered and hummed and worked his arms and shoulders in such a way that he might have been carrying on with his whittling or been performing some mystic ritual known only to skalds.

The faces, nearly in unison, swung back to the chieftain. Asa remembered her mother placing a hand on her father's shoulder and him gently pushing it away. "Well, then," he'd said, "shall we have another game?" And she kept picturing the faces, gaunt and bewildered in the firelight, bobbing first from Jorgen and then to her father and then back again, endlessly, like so much driftwood at the mercy of the tide. How had she not understood all this before?

"I said"—Wenda was speaking again—"why didn't your father act?"

Asa felt her cheeks flush hot. It was only a misjudgment; she could still defend him. "He did act," she began. "He made plans for next summer's crops, and he designed a separate cooking house that would be closer to the storeroom and still catch some wind." Was that really answering the question? "He kept us thinking about the future," she explained. "This has been a very tough winter; a lot of people have died. My father was doing his best—"

"And what was Jorgen doing?"

His worst, was the answer that came to mind. He'd managed to march her father and all of the able-bodied men onto the *Sea Dragon* and shoved it into a stormy sea, leaving him nearly free to take control.

"Or your mother, what did she do?"

Asa rubbed her forehead, shielding her eyes. Images of her mother flashed through the blackness: trying to sit upright though trembling with nausea, overseeing the cooking, directing Jorgen to tell a story—or had that been herself?—but finally giving in to her illness, the sweat and fever fogging her orders.

"They're blind," the woman said, to which Asa nodded, not even looking up. "So you must go back. But not as yourself."

XII

ÞRETTÁN

That night Asa hugged herself into a tight ball, tucked her cloak around her knees and clasped it close to her neck, and lay facing the fire. She'd not been offered a mattress or even so much as a blanket by Wenda. Soon after the woman's cryptic remark, when her white-haired head had begun to nod and her one eyelid had slowly closed over its intimidating orb, she'd watched the woman suddenly startle awake, rise to her feet, and pull herself up into some sort of woven bed suspended from the rafters, the likes of which Asa had never seen. The thick netting had sagged and swayed back and forth for a time with the woman's settling weight, but when she finally fell still her lumpy silhouette could, in the dark cave's smoky haze, have been mistaken for one especially large chunk of drying meat—a chunk of meat that emitted a heedless, whistling snore that only added to Asa's aggravation. So she lay curled between Rune and the fire, catching some warmth from both and thinking glumly that the long day was ending much as it had begun: huddled within a rocky shelter far from home, plagued by thoughts of what the morrow might bring.

When her own eyes finally relented and she gave in to a fitful sleep, Asa dreamed of a stranded whale, a large blue-black one, with one great round pale eye that blinked at her. The whale's hide glistened, bathed as it was in an ethereal light. Sparkling rivulets of seawater traced paths along its creamy throat and sleek flanks. The creature's cavernous breathing, deep and slow, in and then out—as rhythmic as the ocean—pulsed through her blood. For some reason the whale seemed to have flung itself on the shore to wait for her, and as she stood staring up at its immense bulk, it blinked and waited and breathed and waited. She was supposed to do something, but she didn't know what that something was. And as she stood helplessly, squinting up at it in the blazing light, the two ravens came flapping their way into her view, circled the whale, and then landed on its broad, sloping back. There they strutted arrogantly, pecking at its blowhole and demanding in their raven speak (which Asa could understand in her dream) that the whale offer up its eye. *What do you want for it?* they screeched. *What shall we trade you for your eye?* And the water that trickled off the whale was blindingly bright and then she awoke.

At first she lay motionless, her heart kicking against her ribs. Where was she? It seemed to be the sheltered niche at the shore, because a stone wall blocked her view of the ocean and somewhere nearby the two ravens were screaming. But where was Rune? She scanned her surroundings. No, not the shore—inside Wenda's cave. That much was coming back to her. But still, where was Rune? She lifted onto an elbow, trying to think.

A commotion sounded outside the cave—flapping wings and pinging stones—and then he came wandering in, bobbing his head the way he did when he'd found an especially tasty treat. His lips oozed a green foam. "Rune," she called with relief, and he ambled over, hooves lazily scraping the stone, and nuzzled her head. She tried to duck away but, too late, a wet glob was deposited on her scalp. Laughing, she reached up to give him a shove and had to stop short with a pained gasp. The muscles in her shoulders and back had recoiled in protest. That brought another memory: her battle with Jorgen. With bubbling anger she noted the slashes across Rune's neck but also saw that his chest, where the short hairs swirled in damp disorder, had been washed clean of any dried blood. Hearing someone approach, Asa climbed to her feet too suddenly and another spasm gripped her, so that when Wenda entered the cave, the two met as crooked twins.

"Ach! You've not enough winters to be walking like an old woman," Wenda said.

She seemed to be in tremendous good spirits, as changeable as the weather. Rune left Asa to give the empty grain basket a shove with his nose, and that made Wenda laugh.

"Soon enough, soon enough," she said, picking it up and carrying it to the barrel that held the barley. Rune's ears pricked at the vigorous crunch of the scoop biting into the grain. He nickered eagerly as she approached with the filled basket, and in the next instant he was tearing into the mound, his thick black-and-silver mane clouding his face.

It pleased Asa to see him eating so well. That winter she'd often wished to go hungry herself—to offer up her measly bowl of pea soup if it would help—rather than see her old friend suffer. "Thank you," she said to Wenda, "again."

That got her a quick over-the-shoulder glance and a lopsided smile that hinted at secrets. Then Wenda busied herself with the fire, nudging its embers into flames.

The morning view through the cave's crooked mouth showed no rain. Within the sunless gloom shading the opposite side of the fjord she could just pick out the narrow trail that had led here. Certainly they could find their way now. And, anxious to move on, she announced, "We'll be leaving as soon he's finished."

"You will?" Was it doubt or sadness that colored the response?

She had to nod. She'd foolishly followed the old woman here yesterday because she'd been promised a whale. Obviously there was none; she'd been misled for who knew what reason—if *reason* had even had any part in it. So she needed to resort to her previous plan: climb higher into the mountains and search for food there, then return to her clan.

The makeshift rafters with their bounty of dried meats tugged her gaze upward. If Wenda was a generous host—well, there was no need traveling along that path; if she wanted a share she'd boldly have to ask for it. Even then she'd still search for more food before returning to her clan. Who knew how thin this winter could stretch?

"I'm grateful for the shelter and the food. And for bathing his wounds." She indicated Rune. "I'm afraid I was so tired I didn't hear you leave earlier. Is there some work I can do for you before I go—fetch water or gather more firewood, something to pay for your kindnesses?"

Wenda began to smile in preface to her reply. Or so it appeared. Instead the smile widened, pulled the lips thin and bloodless, and contorted them into a grotesque, frozen mask. Slowly the woman lifted her arms, spreading them wide. As if the gesture alone were a voiced command, the ravens came flapping into the cave with powerful whooshing strokes and alit, one upon each arm. Their beaks stabbed the air as the feathers on their heads rose up in a menacing display, and both birds yelled at Asa.

"You wish to pay me, do you? Can you pay for a whale? How much is one worth, would you say? You have no silver coins." Here Wenda raked her head up and down like one of her birds, critically eyeing Asa's full length. "So what would you trade for it?"

"I'm not talking about a whale—"

"Yes, you are!" the woman shrieked, and at that Rune startled sideways, snorting alarm. Her one eye rolled back inside her head. The wrinkled lid fluttered, the narrow slit showed a mucous, yellowy white, and all the while her two black birds hollered at Asa as if she were the cause of the woman's torment.

The skin on Asa's neck prickled and the tingly sensation raced across her shoulders and down her arms. She needed to escape this crazy old woman. *Now.* The shelter and food had been welcomed, but she and Rune risked unknown danger with each passing moment. They had to be on their way.

Wenda's mouth contorted into a new grimace. Her neck spasmed, yanking her head stiffly askew. The one eye continued to shudder and roll until the lid's gossamer folds closed over it. In another raspy breath it popped open. The woman swayed. She seemed not to know where she was and her one eye kept blinking and blinking, trying to find its focus.

The ravens' vocalizations softened at once. Their feathers smoothed and the pair gurgled and mewled quietly, almost contemplatively. One casually preened his—or was it her?—chest while the other trilled an intermittent, single-noted melody. As Wenda steadied herself (and as Asa hesitated, momentarily mesmerized) the birds subtly shifted their prattle into something more distinctive. The raven on her left shoulder—the female, Asa decided, because the bird was slightly trimmer and neat-looking—parted her wings and made a throaty sound that resembled a hammer striking metal. In response, the other bird—the male—emitted a series of emphatic grunts. He let the last grunt expand into a protracted groan. The exchange, nearly a conversation, continued as the woman blinked to awareness. Before long she was cocking her head this way and that and, even though her chest rose and fell with some effort, and her suspended arms trembled, she seemed to understand the birds' percussive litany.

It was all too strange and discomforting for Asa, and, seeing that Rune was finished eating, she sidled over to him and tugged on his forelock, nudging him toward the cave's mouth. "Thank you," she said again, carefully polite. She wouldn't be asking for any of the meats.

Wenda lifted her arms higher, gently flinging the birds upward. The two ravens winged their way once around the cave's upper reaches before obediently exiting. Whatever seizure had overtaken her had vanished. Her mouth opened and closed, tasting the air; an empty swallow rippled her throat. Her thin lips relaxed into place. Her one eye still blinked rapidly, but when her gaze fell upon Asa, it showed recognition along with unexpected good will. This time the smile remained warm. "Are you so easily swayed by an ill wind?" she asked.

Asa stood dumbstruck, neither understanding the question nor conjuring up any proper answer.

"Can you not use your two good eyes," Wenda continued, "to see things as they are—not as people tell you they are—but *as they are*?"

It was like finding herself trapped knee deep in an unseen bog and being asked by a critical onlooker to discuss her situation. She didn't know how the misstep had taken place or why; she just wanted to get out of the suffocating, clammy predicament. "I'm sorry." She measured her words with care, not wanting to irritate the temperamental woman again. "But I'm afraid I don't understand you." Her hand sought for and found Rune's mane and she tugged on it with a subtle urgency. "And, you see, we really must be going . . ."

"And where will you run off to this time, Asa Coppermane?" Wenda's voice was as calm as Asa's, though its odd tenor matched the iciness in her pale blue eye. "Where will you run—nay, *how can* you run—when the people of your clan are trapped within the gluttonous grasp of Jorgen the Younger? Do you not feel the cloak of responsibility on your shoulders? Has all of your father's work been so easily tossed to the winds?" In a dramatic pantomime, she offered her leathery palm, leaned closer, and blew a gust of air across it, a breath that reeked of decay.

Asa was getting nowhere with Rune. He seemed to be entranced by the woman's nonsensical words and stood lock-kneed and unresponsive. "I'm not running away," she countered, still measuring the distance to the entry and jabbing Rune's neck with her thumb. "I'm trying to find food for my clan. If you could kindly manage to share some of your store"—she jerked her head toward the rafters—"I'll carry it to them right away."

Sudden disappointment weighed on Wenda's face. Taken aback and finding herself strangely concerned for the obviously lonely woman, Asa hesitantly added, "I'm certain you could come live with us. . . ."

But before she could finish, Wenda clenched her fists and shook them. "Don't be such a child! You're grabbing for worms when I'm offering you a whale."

The whale again. That was it; she'd had enough. Half-witted or not, the old woman wasn't being coddled any longer. "You keep promising me a whale," Asa retorted. "You lured me here, in fact, with the promise of a whale, but you don't have one." She slapped Rune's neck, startling him into movement toward the cave's mouth. She trailed him with her every sense heightened, gathering up her cloak and stepping cautiously but quickly. "Whales don't fly out of the ocean and come begging to be let in to someone's filthy cave."

Now it was hurt that flashed across Wenda's face. She was human after all, it seemed—not totally without her pride. She started to lift her arms again, exhaled sharply, and dropped them. Indignant, she drew her cloak tightly across her neck and looked away. Asa moved past her.

"Wait."

Rune was already outside the cave, and the ravens must have been tormenting him because she heard an especially provocative *kra* followed by the clatter of scrambling hooves on stone. Somewhat remorseful, she hesitated.

"If your horse can carry provisions, I'll send some meat back with you."

Asa inclined her head. "I would be very grateful for that."

That made the woman swell a little and she immediately set about deciding which meats to pull down. She stroked the fuzz on her bony chin and pondered, pointing to one and ordering Asa to take it but then, just as she had clambered atop a barrel and was reaching for it, maddeningly changing her mind and pointing to another joint or shoulder on the other end of the rafters. When, after an aggravatingly long passage of time, a suitable pile of meat had been assembled, Wenda had to dig for and find two large woolen sacks and a length of thin rope. Rune was brought back into the cave—Asa noted the fjord's lessening gloom; the sun was on the move, and so should they be—leaving the ravens to flap back up to their nest. Wenda, humming now, fitted the rope around Rune's belly and knotted it behind his withers. The flopping tails of the rope were then knotted around the sacks so that one bag fell along each of his shoulders. Into one sack Wenda shoved her generous allotment of mutton, venison, and pork, and in the other she carefully layered a dozen of the drying fishes, arranging them so gently that they might have been still alive.

"Don't leave them in here too long," she advised. "Spread them out in the sun as soon as you get back, or string them near a smoky fire so that they can finish drying." She caught herself, raised a hand, and backed away. "But you already know that, I'm sure."

Asa offered a self-deprecating grimace. "Well, my mother does." That is, if she was still alive. Resolved to believe it so, she added, "She'll be very appreciative as well."

Wenda, who only the previous morning had pronounced Asa's mother dead, remained expressionless. She fussed with the position of the bags, making sure each hung evenly, then grasped the rope behind Rune's shoulder and gave it a testing tug. He staggered sideways and pinned his ears in irritation.

"You don't have a bridle."

"I didn't have time."

A frown creased the old woman's brow as she glanced around

her disheveled cave. "We can fashion something, I suppose, so you can lead him."

Asa stood beside Rune, impatiently scratching the narrow hollow beneath his jaw. "There's no need," she answered. "He'll follow." And at that she felt the pale blue eye appraise them both and felt herself, at least, come up short.

"Ah, loyalty," Wenda said coolly. "An admirable trait . . . and a prime cause of blindness."

Asa swallowed. The cords in her neck tightened and her skin prickled with warning. *All right, time to leave.* "Well, thank you . . . for everything." Hurriedly she nudged Rune out of the cave and onto the trail ahead. "If you ever get lonely," she turned to say, "we're half a day's journey south of here, just beyond three fingers of land." The strong-minded old woman remained at the cave's mouth, her prominent features as wind-worn as the rocks, yet she appeared so fragile and really quite small considering the expanse of the great, gloomy fjord. Surely she'd be better off in the company and care of others. Maybe if she joined Asa's clan she'd take to Ketil. But there was Tora; she posed a problem. Hardly a day passed that Tora didn't start an argument over some imagined slight. Asa couldn't imagine the two of them sharing the same longhouse. Well, she'd made the offer. It was up to the old woman to act on it. Nodding, she said, "Good-bye."

She glanced up at the two ravens perched on the twiggy rim of their huge nest. They were silent for once, their beady brown eyes marking her every move with an eerie intelligence.

Asa never heard Wenda's approach. Incredible, really, since the fjord was so silent, the breeze absent. Propelled by a violent, breathtaking shove, Asa suddenly found herself teetering perilously close to the edge of the precipice. The small woman possessed an unnatural strength.

"What is it you fear?" The words came hissing into Asa's ear. All she could register, though, was the dizzying height and the thought that no one would ever know what had happened to her.

"Is it death? Is it death you fear?"

Asa shook her head. A lie, of course, because she'd already pictured herself splatting onto the jagged rocks so very far below. No, she didn't want to die. Not yet. She held herself very still, fearing the woman would shove her into the air at the slightest provocation.

"But you're afraid of that skald, aren't you? You didn't gallop from your clan to seek food; you galloped to get away from him."

"He was trying to hurt Rune," Asa replied in a voice barely above a whisper.

"He was trying to hurt *you*."

"He has . . . powers," she stammered. "You don't understand. He can make things happen, make people do things."

Wenda jerked her with such force that Asa lost her balance and went tumbling. She thought at first that she was falling down through the air and instinctively she flung out her arms, but instead she smacked the flat stone entry. Though she gasped with the jolt, she felt its reassuring stability beneath her and welcomed life.

In her heart-pounding daze she heard Wenda laughing. Was this all a dream?

"He's not a god," Wenda said. She offered her hand, a gesture Asa pointedly ignored. Gathering herself, she climbed to her feet, shaking off her skirts and gingerly wiping bits of grit from her reddened palms. In her dizzy state the cliff's edge appeared to vibrate, and she staggered a few steps backward.

"Come now," Wenda cajoled, "I promised you a whale and, if you do as I ask, you shall have one." She scurried into the cave, her excited talk temporarily muddied and muted, then emerged with another bulging sack. "We'll need your horse to carry this, too."

Asa shook her head. This was absurd. "No," she replied. "I'm not traveling with you any farther. I can't trust you."

"Of course you can't." Wenda made the statement seem obvious. "You can only trust yourself." She looked over and grinned, her pink tongue waggling across her stubble of brown teeth. "So, are we going?"

XIV FJÓRTÁN

If the old half-wit wanted to follow them back to the clan, then so be it. That had been her opinion when they'd set out. So how, Asa wondered only a short time into their journey, had Wenda managed to shoulder her way into the lead? Asa wasn't going to follow her anywhere except home, and she most definitely wasn't going to believe anything the woman said. Except for that part about not trusting her; *that* she was willing to take as truth.

The woman was certainly a mystery. Too many years living alone had no doubt addled her mind, along with too many years "speaking" with birds. But her cramped, birdlike walk carried her up the trail without mishap, and her singsong mumbling was shot through with happiness. There was no sign now of the violence that had nearly propelled Asa over the cliff, though the memory alone kept her eyeing the steep drop-off.

An ominous scraping sound behind her preceded a clatter of hooves and a grunt, and she turned to find Rune struggling to regain his balance. The woven bags he lugged made the narrow trail doubly difficult and he had to move carefully, his nose sweeping the ground, his eyes large and darkened in concentration.

Back and forth his ears flicked, marking the undulating pitch of Wenda's murmuring, the crunching grit of the granite path, and the irregular ping and pop of threads snagged on stumpy-fingered branches.

Turning back, Asa nearly collided with Wenda, who had stopped to ponder a cleft in the fjord. Asa followed her gaze up to where a faint foot trail within the cleft rose abruptly. "We'll go this way," Wenda said, pointing. And without so much as a glance backward she clambered atop a boulder, then nimbly stepped across to another.

"No." It surprised her that the word had come out so vehemently.

From her vantage point Wenda looked over her shoulder.

"We didn't come that way," Asa said.

"This way's faster. It's steeper at first, but then as straight as the raven flies."

Asa hesitated for just a moment, weighing the facts. She needed to get back to her clan as fast as possible, not only because she carried precious foodstuffs, but also because she'd been away for far too long. The memory of her mother's feverish face stabbed her with guilt. Yet . . . the mountains were unfamiliar, and no matter what Wenda promised, Asa wasn't following her. "No," she said again, firmly. "We'll go this way." She made a vague gesture toward the path hugging the fjord. Wenda shrugged and returned, this time falling in behind, and they tramped on.

Retracing the narrow fjord seemed to go faster than yesterday. Was it because she was headed home, with enough food to satiate the starved bellies of her people, or because she'd finally fled the confines of Wenda's weird, debris-riddled cave?

With each step closer to the ocean the gloom of the fjord lessened. The sea was at first a glimpsed jewel, its blue-green facets dazzling the eye, and then, gradually, a vast entity that at once inspired and overwhelmed. When the path finally dropped them onto the crunching litter of the shore, she felt some of the worry fall from her shoulders. They'd made it back to solid ground, to a world that was familiar to her and, more important, connected to her home. Rune seemed to share her relief. Compressing a sigh into a rumbling grunt, he shook his head so exuberantly that the vibration traveled the length of his body and sent the bags jumping and flopping in their own celebration.

That's when the two ravens soared into view. Asa imagined they'd remained in their nest, leisurely watching the plodding humans and their horse slowly circumnavigate the fjord, before winging their way directly across the dark waters. One of the birds spiraled downward to alight upon the same rock where it had awakened Asa the previous day, but the other bird flew along the coastline and disappeared. The raven on the rock, rather than taking up its usual scolding, folded it wings neatly and stood watching Asa with uncanny interest. She turned away.

The sun glared cold and white from a cloudless sky. Across the shore the wind came rushing; it tousled the hair around their heads and receded. Upon its return it playfully nipped their reddened cheeks; it poked its icy fingers inside their collars; and it fanned Rune's tail into a black whirligig that slashed the air with the sound of whipping branches. This was a wind full of life, but it played a lonely game: The beach remained barren.

Cuckoo Month had always delivered gusty winds, but it was supposed to deliver warmer days as well. It was a time when the sun charmed the land into bringing forth life: green sprouts that blossomed and grew heavy with fruit; razor-winged birds that painted the cliffs with their nests and worked tirelessly to feed their raucous offspring; long-suffering cows and sheep and pigs that emerged from their dark byres to reproduce themselves in miniature. As she thought on the traditional order of her world, the wind smacked her face. She shielded her eyes and scanned the shore in both directions. Yes, the sun was shining and the day was noticeably warmer than those that had come before. But where was the new life? She saw no signs of it, and wondered if it was truly absent or if she'd grown blind to its possibilities.

The shrill two-syllable call of a bird sounded from somewhere down the shore. A tern? That was just the sign she needed. One tern would mean many terns, which would mean winter was finally ending. She had to go see.

Trying to quell the excitement bubbling inside, she spun toward Wenda. The woman immediately waved her on. "These old bones are going to rest awhile. You go have a look and we'll catch up," she said, indicating Rune, who was nosing through some seaweed. Asa strode away in search of the strange call.

It was difficult to blend speed and silence as she traveled with one ear cocked, especially when the wind played around her head, alternately whispering and whistling and making it difficult to hear. But it had to have been a tern; she was certain of it. And she allowed herself to recall the summer when hundreds of nests had cupped thousands of delicious eggs. The nimblest boys had clambered up the cliffs to claim a great number of them. Helgi and Thidrick should be able to manage it this year. The way her mouth was watering she might just climb the cliffs herself if she spotted even a single egg. That happy thought buoyed her along, and she felt the sun putting a little more effort into warming her shoulders. The wind quieted, and she caught the tern's distinctive call again and hurried after it.

Her eyes scanned the cliffs as she traced the narrow shore. Though the winter's storms had scoured them with rain and wind, the rocks still remained streaked with bird droppings, and here and there a crevice stubbornly clung to the tattered remnants of a nest. A festive spurt of rainwater shot down the steep face of one gray bluff. Gaining ground, it surged along a narrow depression in the wet sand to meld with the sea. Among the surf's bubbles floated a thick, leafy strand of brown seaweed, and Asa dragged it to higher ground. She'd throw it across Rune's back when he got there and take it home to the other horses—if they were still around—and the pregnant cow. Caught among the leaves was a pretty shell, mottled a brownish purple. That made her think of Wenda and her collection of colorful stones, and she clutched the smooth, weighty shell in her palm, musing on the strange morning.

For all her wildly variant moods, Wenda yet held a fascination. Of course Asa was wary of her now; she'd very nearly been murdered by her, hadn't she?

Or had she? She distinctly remembered smacking the stone entry to the cave. But had she been held over the fjord's lip? Or had her imagination made more of the tussle—no, not even that, only a jostle, really—than was true? The woman spoke in such riddles that recalling the subject or order of conversations was difficult. *What are you afraid of?* came back to her. *What are you afraid of?* If Wenda had really threatened to kill her, though, why was she still alive?

That slowed her step. Had she conjured demons out of shadows, maliciousness out of a frown? Wenda had given shelter to both her and Rune; she'd fed them, and now here she was sending her own food stores back to Asa's clan. It was all good, all good. Until the one eye rolled to white and . . .

No, she wasn't going to ponder that.

The tern's two-syllable call sounded again, directly above her now, and she tilted her head excitedly to see . . . a raven. One of Wenda's ravens, by the looks of it. The huge black bird teetered on an exposed root, balancing against the updrafts. Seeing her watching, he lifted his shoulders and made the false call again.

She'd been tricked! For a moment Asa stood motionless, her chest rising and falling, heat coursing through her blood. Then, in one violent move she pitched the shell at the bird. It smugly lifted into flight, not the least alarmed. It flew northward and she marked its diminishing silhouette until it dipped beyond a prominent bluff. Rune and Wenda had not yet caught up so, after heaving a few stones into the ocean for good measure, Asa resolutely walked back to meet the pair.

That took longer than expected because she ended up retracing every one of her tracks. What had kept them? Rounding the last promontory, prepared to urge them to their feet, she couldn't believe what she saw: Wenda was tossing the dried meats into the ocean! Stunned, Asa watched her reach into one of the bags, lug out a chunk, and, teetering slightly with the effort, fling it into the air. The meat plunked into the sea with the weight of a rock.

"No! Stop that!" she cried as she broke into a run. The woman had to have heard her; Rune lifted his head. But Wenda continued pulling the meats and dried fishes from the bags and methodically sailing them over the water.

Asa barreled into her so roughly that Wenda fell backward onto the sand. That brought one of the ravens flapping to the scene, screaming indignation.

"What are you doing?" Asa's scream overpowered the bird's. "You've ruined everything!" Hastily she peered into the bags. The supply was down to one green-tinged mutton loin and a few splintered fishes.

From her disheveled position Wenda whined. "I was sending

food for your whale. You don't expect him to come for nothing, do you?"

Asa clenched her fists as a foul oath sputtered on her lips. She stamped the sand, stamped it a second time, and spun around in utter fury. Then, depositing a glare as harsh as a blow on the old woman—who dared to blink in feigned innocence—she sprang onto Rune's back. Her fingers laced his mane and her heels pummeled his sides and they bolted away.

XV
FIMTÁN

Jorgen lowered his end of the wide, rough-hewn plank to the ground, opened his fingers, and let it drop with a rigid thud. The body carried upon it slid toward him so that the shrouded head just kissed his boots. This gesture of obeisance, even after the fact, moved him slightly. How different things might have been. If only she'd recognized his talents while she yet breathed, their lives might have intertwined to mutual benefit. Tantalizing possibilities, as heady as mead, tickled his senses, until he noticed Ketil waiting dumbly at the other end of the plank.

"What are you staring at?" he scolded. That startled Ketil into dropping the plank with a bang and stumbling backward. Jorgen set his heel against the head's crown and pushed, trying to shove the bundled body back into place. The neck, not yet stiffened, lolled from beneath the pressure and his boot slipped off. No surprise. Even in death the woman was spineless. Rolling his eyes, he walked to the other end and elbowed the useless cripple out of the way. He bent down and jerked the remains squarely onto the board.

"They smell of cheese," Ketil whispered into his ear. A

wide-eyed child in an old man's body, he stood transfixed by the row of bundles, seemingly fearful that his least stray movement would cause the nearest to tumble atop him. "Who'd have thought?"

Cheese? How could one possibly identify cheese from this rotting assault on the senses? The man was a fool—a cripple and a fool—and Jorgen rose abruptly to deliver his most withering glare. "You must go now. I have the ritual to perform." Ketil only too happily backed through the doorway, stumbling as he spun, and hurried away with the glazed look of a frightened hare. His hobbling gait sent crackling fractures across the path's muddy skim of ice.

Jorgen moved to the doorway to watch Ketil's departure. He rubbed his dripping nose and winced when the heel of his hand met his swollen lip. The split flesh had been throbbing for two days, persistently and maddeningly recalling his struggle in the other byre. For all of those two days he'd firmly held the memories at bay. Now, allowing himself to remember that night increased the pain and sent it worming its way through his insides.

What had happened to her? One after another, dramatic story lines uncoiled in his mind. She and her horse had tumbled over a cliff: He visualized his own arm reaching down to pull her to safety; he felt her nestle against his chest, the heat of her small body soaking into his. In another calamitous scenario she'd fallen sick and wandered alone and feverish through the mountain forests, lost. This one gnawed holes of worry in his belly, especially with icy rain pounding the earth and cold winds tearing through the trees.

Why hadn't she understood his plans for her? Why had she challenged him with such impudence? It was all so infuriating.

To ease his stomachache he dug through his pouch for the last of the angelica roots. Touching them brought forth another memory: He'd collected them last summer at the damp edge of the outfield where he'd been watching her. Her copper hair had fallen loose from its braid that day, and the wind, with a familiar hand, had lifted it from her shoulders and spun it across her cheek and made her laugh.

Working the spongy root between his teeth, he thought about that laugh. It was a rarity, impulsive and infectious. She'd shared it with few others, and never with him. A bitter taste filled his mouth. The root's usual soothing warmth failed to materialize, and he swallowed the pulpy fragments without any faith that they could dull his ache.

Where was she?

If he could just get a rope around one of those wretched horses, he could ride out looking for her. He'd be able to find her and save her; he'd make her understand. And his skin warmed with the vision of the two of them returning astride, her arms locked around his waist in a grateful embrace. Reflexively he closed his eyes and sucked in a breath. Truth be known, that was the least satisfying of his fantasies, because he'd never thrown a leg over the back of a horse.

He heard the maddening creatures now—though he still

couldn't see them—crunching their careless way among the trees, noisily paying him no heed. They skirted the settlement's clearing continually, looking for her but leery of him and any others he sent to coax them in. They taunted him, they did.

He laced his fingers, turned them inside out, and stretched them to the breaking point, focusing his anger. One day soon he'd see their butchered bodies roasting over a fire. This he vowed. Their bodies and that of that runty old dun horse too, the one that had struck at him so purposefully and painfully—if the bony thing was even still alive, and if it dared to return. All three horses that defied him would eventually get what they deserved, and so would she, for that matter, and that would teach her to run off.

Yet . . . all the while that his blood was churning thicker and hotter, he heard a delicate voice in his mind crying, *Help me! Help me!* He searched through his pouch for another of the angelica roots, but they were gone. He pressed a fist to his stomach and sagged against the doorframe, thankful at least for the cold air buffeting his face.

In the stark wintry light the longhouse sat solid and secure, an anchored haven amid the wildly angular mountains at its back. The smoke rising from the roof hole was snatched away by the wind, but the sod roof itself, its silver turf shivering, appeared intact. Only a few leaks inside required someone's attention; a particularly annoying one had pinpointed his own mattress, but that was no longer a concern. He'd abandoned it. He watched spare drops steadily patter the door-slab, painting it a shiny ocean color. Above the door, just under the overhanging fringe, was a drooping pine bough. A frivolous ornamentation, fairly fresh and girlishly cheerful, yet it soothed him. The pine tree outlasted the worst of winters, ever green, and so would he.

He inhaled the freshly cleansed air with new spirit. The clan was his now, finally and entirely. Its spineless leader was drowned; his spineless wife was dead. Things would be different. They were, in fact, already different. Only last night, when the woman's breathing had rattled to an end beside the fire, and the others had gathered around in silence, he'd slipped into the bed-closet once shared by her and her husband. As his heart thumped excitement, he'd lowered himself onto the straw mattress, fully aware that his shoulders and hips oh-so-naturally filled the hollows left by the chieftain. And, lying on that chieftain's mattress in the dark, what visions he'd had! Certain places, he'd learned from his father, held invisible power that could, with immense concentration and unusual skill, be donned like a cloak. This room was one of those places, and behind his closed eyes swirled more intoxicating colors than any he'd experienced.

It was a bold move, even he would admit to that, but one a true leader made without hesitation. Through the wooden wall he'd heard their murmurings, and he'd opened his eyes once when the door creaked ajar to find Tora observing him with her slitted green eyes. Always before she'd looked upon him with barely concealed disfavor, as did the other stupid women, but now her eyes showed new consideration. To add to his intoxication he believed that if he only crooked a finger and gestured, Tora would come to him. But it wasn't her he wanted.

The next morning, this selfsame morning, he'd made certain to arise before any of them and to arrange himself beside the prone body of the chieftain's wife. He'd sat there fiddling with his bear tooth amulet, waiting for the others to discover him in ritual attendance, when he'd noticed the woman's finger twitch. The insufferable creature was still alive! At death's door she was turning and threatening him with a wagging finger! He had had no choice then but to lean through the darkness and lay his hands upon her more forcefully, one across her mouth and the other across her nose. When he'd pinched the nostrils together, she hadn't even struggled. She was weak; they were all weak.

For some time he masked her bony face with his hands and prayed rather vaguely that the afterlife would welcome her. His prayers were unfocused because his thoughts were springing about the room, marking all that was now his; eagerly his eyes followed. Whenever his gaze returned to the task his hands performed, he assured himself it was in the best interests of the clan. What he did was no different, really, than when the weakest animals were slaughtered at summer's end because there was only enough food to support the strong.

As he slumped against the doorframe, his thumb stroked the knobby hilt of the old sword he wore. It was a cast-off, its dull blade heavily pitted and, in fact, snapped short. But it still threatened; he saw its worth in the faces of the surviving clan members. When they'd awakened and found him at the dead woman's side with the shortened sword belted at his waist, he'd noted the looks they'd exchanged and his chest swelled. As it did now. It had taken most of a lifetime, but he was finally getting the respect he deserved. No longer was he a collared dog performing tricks, but a leader, a bold leader, one who didn't hesitate to mete out punishment as needed. Thidrick could cradle his ear and wail in his mother's lap the rest of the day if he liked, but he'd learned the consequences of touching this sword.

Yes, the clan was his. Things were and would be different. Tonight he'd ease any doubts about his leadership with the small cask of beer he'd discovered in the bed-closet. He'd stop their questions with a story of how Odin, a god both mercurial and merciful, swallowed weak leaders upon stormy seas. It's what gods did.

XVI SEXTÁN

The sun had just dipped behind the green-black mountains when Asa and Rune came upon the familiar sight of her clan's fishing huts and the row of upturned boats, long unused.

Almost home now, and what did she have to show for her rash venture? A rope of kelp, a chunk of meat, some fish. A bounty, considering the barren storeroom. She'd be welcomed. But a nagging sense of failure shadowed her. What, really, had changed?

Rune angled his face away from the gust that blasted the shore, and she wriggled her legs beneath the bags, seeking the warmth of his body. The evening sky glowed a luminous white, like an eggshell held against fire, though bands of rippled clouds, each edged a fierce orange, threatened.

Then there was Jorgen. Her scabbed lip burned at his name. Her bruised shoulder throbbed. She felt her jaw tighten. What had he told the others about her disappearance? Lies, no doubt—lies that had needlessly worried her mother. Wenda was right. She was only a little girl who'd run off in the night, abandoning her clan. A fool.

Another gust lifted Rune's mane and whipped her own hair across her face. In its whistling she detected a faint, mournful call. Human? Animal? She halted him, cupping her hands to both ears to listen. There it was again, coming from the forest that rose above them, and filled with such fear that her heart squeezed. She should help.

But she was so close to home and the wind was growing ever stronger. The weather was changing. Closing her eyes, hoping not to hear it, she waited. Rune pawed the crunching sand. Surf splashed the rocks and receded, gurgling. Teasing gusts hummed and faded.

Nothing.

Relieved, she bumped Rune's sides, urging him on, when the wail sounded again. Her eye swung toward a tumble of boulders and brush fringing a high stand of pines. It came from a calf, she was certain, and her mind raced to make sense of that. Had their heavily pregnant cow gotten out of the byre? And if so, what was she doing this far from the settlement? The call repeated, too pitiful to ignore, and she nudged Rune away from the shore, allowing him to pick an upward passage between and around the rocks, decaying logs, and dense stands of brush. It was difficult going, especially with the fading light and their weaving approach. When it seemed they must be steps from discovering the poor creature, two ravens scrambled past, flapping and squawking. She grimaced. Wenda's ravens, no doubt. Were they following her? And what mischief were they up to now?

Rune plowed blindly through another thicket of tangled brush and emerged in a concealed clearing and nearly on top of the clan's lone cow. Listlessly nosing through a brown mat of pine needles, she barely flicked an ear at their arrival. Her newborn calf, all angular bones and rumpled hair, fretted at her side. He butted the slack udder with his wet nose, let out a mournful bawl as he danced sideways, and tried again, all the while swishing his tail in anxious jerks.

The calf was alive and well! Their herd had doubled! A fiery determination to protect the pair hurried Asa from Rune's back. She dragged the ropy kelp from his shoulders and piled it beneath the hungry cow. As she straightened, an unnaturally bright fleck of white on the other side of the clearing caught her eye. Another calf? The cow must have been carrying twins. Their herd had tripled! Mindful of the slippery mountainside, she hurried over to examine the speckled newborn sleeping in an awkward heap.

Shock trampled her excitement. Not only was the calf already dead, it had no eyes. Its bloody sockets gaped blindly at the world. That could be the work of ravens. They'd been known to kill young animals by the most horrible practice of pecking out their eyes. Still . . . stark images flashed through her mind: the sightless fish suspended outside Wenda's cave, the woman's own hollow eye cavity. Wenda's pointed questions echoed: *What would you do to rescue your clan? Would you give up an* eye*?* An uncomfortable ripple along her spine suggested a connection. She'd not escaped Wenda yet.

A loud *kra!* made her flinch, and one of the ravens swooped past to land on the calf's carcass, triumphant. Immediately it began pecking at the empty socket, teasing away a stringy piece of flesh and gobbling it down. That emboldened the second raven to join in.

How dare they? This defenseless calf had been her clan's future. She screamed and lunged, sending them into hasty flight, then stood over the calf protectively. At the very least there'd be some meat in the cooking pot tonight.

But first she needed to get the cow and her surviving calf into the safety of the byre. How could someone have been so careless as to leave the door open? That was Jorgen's doing, no doubt, and as disquieting recollections invaded her, she detected a noise in the forest and froze. Rune's ears pricked. Silently she moved to his side, ready to jump on his back and return to the open shore where they could gallop. A twig broke, some dried leaves crackled, and Rune gave a loud whinny. Answering whinnies ricocheted through the trees. Her father's horses! More good news.

And hard on that joy: fear. Jorgen wanted to kill them, especially Rune. She had to face him, she knew, but Rune didn't. For now he'd be safer in the forest. As fast as she could, she unknotted the rope and let the bags fall. Amongst the trees, unseen hooves pawed anxiously at the earth. Rune whinnied again and the echoing calls returned.

Gently she laid her hand on his wounds; their slight stickiness left only a faint webbing of red on her palm. "Be careful," she whispered, and slapped his rump, sending him off. He bounded a few strides upward, then came to a halt to look over his shoulder. From beneath his shaggy black forelock his eyes questioned. "It's all right." She flung her arms in the air. "Go." Bunching his haunches, he clambered eagerly up the rocky incline, nickering between grunts. When he disappeared into the forest, such an overwhelming sense of loss swept her that she had to close her eyes and turn away.

The damp winds surging up the slope carried the smell of wood smoke and a promise of warmth. Night was near, and it was time to get the cow and her calf to safety. Time to get under a roof herself.

Freeing the rope from the bags, she looped it around the cow's thin neck, careful not to let it cut into the dangling flap at her throat. She gave a gentle tug, which the cow blatantly ignored. She tugged harder, but the cow continued nosing the kelp. Her calf, meanwhile, having found a teat with milk, was suckling hungrily, pausing on occasion to butt his mother's flank for more.

She sighed in frustration. Horses were so much more agreeable than cows. How was she going to goad these two toward the byre? To add to her distress, a dank gloom was creeping across the clearing and the not-too-distant hiss of rain sounded high above. There was no time to waste. She choked up on the rope with both hands, leaned into her heels, and pulled hard. The cow twisted her head obstinately, not budging. Rain suddenly engulfed the mountain with a deafening roar. Muddy rivulets began churning down the slope, soaking her boots. She gave one more hard tug, lost her balance, and fell. Gravel bit her hand as soppy earth soaked her skirt.

That was it. Exasperated, she yanked the rope from the cow, hoisted the dead calf onto her shoulders, managed to grab the bags, and, stumbling under the soggy burden of her increasingly clingy clothes, made her way down from the forest and homeward. The cow and her calf would have to fend for themselves until morning. She was cold and tired, and now drenched as well, and she wanted to sleep under a roof. And she wanted to see her mother.

That guilty desire pushed her even faster through the deluge: She'd been away too long; she'd tarried with the animals too long. The fevered pronouncement Wenda had made upon their meeting—that her mother was already dead—tormented her mind. She tried drowning it in mumbled prayers to Freyja, her mother's favorite goddess, and hurried on.

Out of breath, her legs spongy, she reached the settlement. The rain eased, and a few glittery stars poked through a twilight sky mottled with drifting gray clouds. Everywhere water roared across the earth to rejoin the sea. She was more than ready to rejoin her clan. Readjusting her load and kicking at the sopping hem of her cloak, she trudged down the last rise.

In the distance the longhouse door opened. A greeting rose in her throat until she recognized Jorgen and she froze in place, praying to meld with the darkened hillside at her back. She hadn't planned on encountering him out here.

Her blood thudded along her neck, her tongue thickened, and

her eyeballs grew chill because she didn't dare even to blink. She watched him jerk his head in a funny way, sniffing at something, looking for something. Finally, after an unbearable while, he retreated inside the longhouse and pulled the door closed after him. Waters still rushed across the earth, noisily returning home, but she couldn't move.

Hating herself, she stood undecided. Her mother was mere steps away. But so was Jorgen.

A few latent raindrops, fat and hard, pelted her head. Yet she stood. A flash of lightning stripped the land naked, startling her to momentary blindness, and when the land fell black again she bolted clumsily toward the nearest shelter: the abandoned byre holding the clan's dead. It would have to do for now.

She half expected an unhappy *draugr* to knock her flat when she entered, but only a rotten odor slapped her face. Not daring to proceed further, she sank to the earthen floor just inside the door and waited for her eyes to adjust to the gloom.

The cloudburst pounded the sod then, as before, abruptly passed on. The steady *drip-drip-drip* of water punctuated the ensuing silence.

As the gloom receded the dead slowly appeared. A mute audience, they stretched away in a neat row, side by side, heads abutting the opposite wall, shapes differing only in the dim color and weave of their blankets. The farther bundles seemed flattened somehow, as if the unhoused souls, tired of waiting for burial, were tugging their decaying bodies into the ground unnoticed.

They had been Einarr, Systa, and her own brother, Harald, there in the oat-colored blanket her mother had woven. The first three to die, though with so many passing it was hard to keep the order straight. Surrounded by so much death, she became acutely aware of her heavy breath warming her cold lips.

Nearer were the bundled forms of Kolla and her shy daughter Ragna, and still nearer, the slender remains of her other brother, Magnus. A bright vision of his freckled face offering a gap-toothed smile sprang to mind. Always laughing, he'd been her father's favorite from the day he was born, and when he'd died, her father had retreated to the bed-closet and not come out for two entire days. Magnus's loss, she believed, had made it easier for her father to step onto the *Sea Dragon* and steer it into the storm.

She pressed her chin onto her knees. She'd not cried for any of them, even her own brothers, and had stoically swallowed the pain their deaths delivered. Death was part of life. And yet . . . and yet it seemed there'd been far too many deaths of late, and that they'd begun weighing inside her like so many stones. She shifted position and drew a difficult breath.

All the while that her eyes were passing back and forth over the bundles, she knew she was pointedly ignoring the nearest one, the newest one, the only bundle in the row free of dust and leaf litter. The only form wrapped in a beautiful madder-red blanket and pinned with her mother's filigreed, gold-and-silver brooch. Its two gripping beasts, eternally entangled, glinted even in the dark.

Clasping her knees tighter, Asa forced herself to look. Tears brimmed. Her mother's death wasn't unexpected, she scolded; and yet, childishly, she felt cheated. She'd never again feel her mother's smooth, calloused hand cupping her chin; never trade good-natured teasing with her; never witness her mother's delight in a double fistful of purple foxgloves dangling on their stalks. All of which she might have had if she hadn't galloped away in the middle of the night and left her mother to die alone. The tears rose further and trembled upon her lashes. She bit her lip, blinked rapidly, angrily, and fought them away. Digging her chin harder into her knees, she recalled every last thing that she loved about her mother and mentally pinned those memories to her shroud, that her mother might remember them also and smile in her spirit world.

Later, when she'd gone numb even to the odors in the cold byre, she sat thinking how everything had gone wrong and she arranged much of the blame around her own shoulders. Long ago she should have seen how lost her father was and how sick her mother was; they'd just hidden their needs so well. And what had she done? She'd galloped off to save Rune and, all right, to seek a little food for the clan, but had been talked (by a fool!) into setting her sights on a whale—a whale, of all things! (And who, really, was the fool?) If only she'd kept her eyes fixed on the ground, gathered some roots or some nuts, taken smaller, safer steps, maybe then she would have returned in time to save her mother. Or at least returned in time to give her a farewell kiss, to prevent her from dying alone.

Now she herself was left truly alone. Her mother and brothers were dead; her father was gone and Rune was gone. She had no one to help her and, worse, though separated by dark and distance, she sensed Jorgen's malicious, manipulative presence. Who knew what he was up to?

Hah! She did know what he was up to: He was taking over leadership of the clan. And with her mother dead, he'd probably already assumed her father's seat of honor beside the fire. That twisted her belly. How was she going to live here? She heaved a sigh as Wenda's words came back to her: *Has all of your father's work been so easily tossed to the winds? Yes,* she answered bitterly, *as easily as smoke*.

It seemed ages since she'd slurped down Wenda's mussel stew; the warm broth would certainly have been welcomed now. Her mouth watered involuntarily. What about the meats left in the bags? Without having to stir too much, she managed to fumble through them.

A lone mutton loin, as heavy and as hard as a rock, lay inside the first bag. It would require a lot of boiling. The dried fish might be palatable so she blindly reached into the second bag. Her fingers met not food but something thick and soft and, even without being able to see it, she knew it was the blue cloak she'd worn in Wenda's cave. At least she could be warm; that was something. Hastily she peeled off her wet cloak and wrapped herself inside the blue one. The garment was nothing short of magical in easing her shivering at once.

Reaching into the last bag she discovered the partially dried fishes. She tore one apart and teased the still tender flesh from the bones. The meat flaked on her tongue and quieted her stomach. Her back unknotted and, with warmth oozing through her body, she gave in to sleep.

She had no idea how much time had passed when she was startled awake by the sound of steps approaching the byre. She held her breath, her heart thumping. Jorgen! It had to be him; no one else dared enter here. She was trapped.

Fastening her eyes in the direction of the door, though she could barely make it out in the darkness, she waited. Another step, muffled by mud, and then another. Slow, hesitant. What was he up to? A whiffle, akin to an animal's breath, came just on the other side of the wall at her back; it was followed by a low, questioning nicker. Rune.

Exhaling in relief, she thanked the gods it wasn't Jorgen, though it would be soon enough. Already she discerned slender strips of gray light across the floor. She climbed to her feet and carefully pushed the byre door open. Rune shoved his head against her, nickering concern.

"Ssh . . . ssh," she soothed, cupping her hand, stiff with cold, over his muzzle and pushing him backward. The mountains stood silhouetted against a fading sky. Day was coming. Jorgen would be coming.

She gazed toward the longhouse. Did she have a place there anymore? Did she have a place anywhere?

She continued to calm Rune with caresses. What should she do?

Feed her clan. That's what she had set out to do. And she plunged back inside the byre to gather up the dead calf. Quietly, she crossed to the longhouse and laid the body on the stone door-slab. Rune watched with pricked ears.

Next she needed to get the cow and surviving calf back to their byre. The rain had stopped, and if the pair weren't ambling their way homeward they were most likely in the same brushy mountainside shelter where she'd left them. She ducked into the small byre once more to grab the bags. There she hesitated. On an impulse she knelt beside the raised planks supporting a shrouded body and swept her hand beneath them. There it was: a bit of cheese, horribly moldy by its odor. She pulled it out, dropped it in the bag containing her wet cloak, and searched for more of Jorgen's selfish hoard. In a matter of minutes she discovered a pouch of what felt like nuts, a rather hefty bag of barley, dozens of tubers she didn't recognize, the molting head of a long-dead fish, and the charred remains of some partially plucked bird wrapped in cloth. The cloth felt rather slimy in her hand; the meat was definitely spoiled. She stuffed it all inside the bags and was ready to leave—Rune was pawing all too noisily on the door-slab—when she hesitated again. She had to let Jorgen know his stab at leadership wasn't going uncontested.

Returning to her mother, Asa carefully unfastened the gold-and-silver brooch and lifted the blanket from her face. The waxy image, bereft of her mother's spirit, stirred little pain in her. Carefully she rolled the blanket back on either side, revealing her mother's hands clasped across her chest. With a shivery thrill Asa tore a piece from one of the dried fishes and tucked it between her mother's hands. When Jorgen returned, he'd find all of his food gone. That made her smile. Let him think her mother, a chieftain's wife, had eaten it all and had even found her own; let him think she was a *draugr*, one of the walking dead. And let him tremble for all the evil he had done.

XVII
SJAUTÁN

A thick coastal fog muted such details as branches, speckles, or crevices. That tumble of boulders resembled the place where she'd found the cow last night, but the longer she searched, the more she suspected she was on the wrong mountainside. Rearranging the beaded blue cloak around her shoulders—how amazingly warm it was!—she whistled softly for Rune. Fog swirled through the brush, like damp smoke seeking kindling, but other than the muffled lapping of the surf below, she didn't hear a sound. No matter. He'd just wandered off. Best thing to do now was climb higher and figure out where she was.

She leaned into the effort, her clouded breath mimicking the drifting fog, and reached an open space nearer the top. Stands of white-trunked birch trees gave way to a thicker pine forest blanketing the rising slope. She still couldn't see much, couldn't get her bearings, but in searching the area she came across a picture-stone, fully the size of a man, silhouetted against the gray sky.

Picture-stones were rare; she'd only known the one on the whale-nosed bluff north of their village, so she approached this one with great curiosity.

Carvings ornamented it from top to bottom. They'd been dug into the rock some time ago, for the lines had been softened by weather and in places cradled bits of damp green mosses and lichens. She trailed her fingertips over the beautiful illustrations, catching droplets of condensation that rolled down her wrist. With a quickening heart she began to sense that the night-chilled stone held a story as momentous as any Jorgen had ever told. While fruited trees crowned the top, embracing robust animals and thatched houses, below and around them wound an enormous, flat-headed dragon that flicked its tongue at one house while stretching its claws toward another. Menace or protector? Rather boldly, she tapped its tail.

Squiggly lines buttressed more fruit trees—furrows? waves?—but beneath them were three straight lines, quite barren. She passed over some incised hatches and dots, symbols that explained the story, she knew, though that magic was known only to skalds. For her the stone held its silence.

Farther down she touched a ship leaping over ocean waves. Men rowed vigorously. Their leader, standing in the prow, pointed toward the horizon. But here the lines describing the sea stretched on and on, and as she followed the turbulent pattern around the side and then to the back of the stone, the men left in the boat seemed to shrink in comparison.

A crunching split the morning's fog-shrouded stillness and she looked down to find a spattering of rock chips and dust beneath lines that were powdery white and new. They reminded her of the pale inner bark of a tree freshly exposed by the bite of an axe. Somebody, it seemed, had recently carved new designs, and she bent to study them more closely.

At the edge of the undulating lines, racing into nothingness, galloped a horse. The girl on his back wore no head cloth and her windblown hair unfurled in long ribbons. She carried a sword in one upraised hand.

A girl warrior? Who was she? How long ago had she lived, and what had happened to her? And . . . who was commemorating her now?

The faint, distant cry of a seabird, carried on a freshening wind, distracted her. The fog was breaking up, and as she turned away from the stone she found herself gradually falling under the hypnotic spell of the ocean's cold blue-gray expanse. It stretched into the distance until it met with an equal expanse of watery blue sky. Both appeared endless, timeless. They had always been and would always be. She shifted position and, as her boot crunched the stone chips again, she became aware of the mountain beneath her. Immense. Immoveable. Unchangeable. The mountain and the sky and the ocean would be here long after she was gone, and she suddenly felt as small as the men in the boat, as inconsequential as a breath of wind. As if to mock her, a gust whipped the hair across her eyes, temporarily blinding her. She brushed it aside, clamping it to her cheek, and looked at the picture-stone anew. It, and the people on it—their images at least—would pass all the days, forever and ever, here with the sky and mountain and sea. A hundred winters from now they would still be rowing, pointing, galloping. A thrill rippled through Asa. Wouldn't that be something? To slip from life's bounds and meld with the earth, to slow one's breathing and become timeless.

More birdcalls punctured the silence, though this time they didn't come from the sea. These were the hoarse cries of ravens. Again? Were they following her? Mocking her? And just as she thought it, the familiar pair flapped into sight, circled above her, and then alit on a shrub, bending the bough perilously close to the ground with their combined weight. They bobbed and preened and snapped their bills, all the while pretending not to watch her, though she knew, just *knew*, that their beady brown eyes marked her every move. As moments passed she got a strong sense that they were waiting for something—or someone—and that gave her a prickly, unsettled feeling.

Asa held her breath and listened. Just when her growing impatience was pushing her to continue looking for Rune and the cow, she heard someone coming and spotted Wenda's hunched figure climbing the same path she'd taken. Asa had no choice but to wait now, though her irritation with the old woman stiffened her jaw.

Maybe she should run and hide. She was younger, faster. But even as her heart kicked and her toes lifted slightly, she knew it would be useless. The ravens would find her, even in the wildness of these mountains they would pick her out, and they'd communicate her whereabouts to Wenda, and the chase would never end. Besides, she was done running.

And so she waited, while the breeze whipped her hair, stinging her face, and the emerging sun nudged her around. On impulse she picked up one of the larger stone chips and fiddled with it, noting the roughness between her fingers, savoring its heft. She'd keep this one piece, she decided, and think about the stone's carvings later. Maybe someone from her clan would remember who the girl on the horse was.

In between these skittering thoughts Asa shielded her eyes and checked Wenda's progress. As the old woman neared, Asa pulled herself tall and glared.

Raspy breaths preceded the woman. Understandable, since it was quite a climb. Admirable, even. Wenda staggered close and grasped the stone with the ferocity of a drowning swimmer clawing at a rope. Her chest rose and fell with her sucking inhalations. Her head lolled forward and her one eye closed tight, and Asa thought she was about to faint. But Wenda seemed to be concentrating on something instead, and as her breathing slowed, she opened her eye and found the two ravens hunched on their bough. Immediately the birds began chattering. Wenda didn't move. She stood rooted, one mottled hand still clutching the stone, the other wrapped around the strap of her satchel.

When it seemed they might pass the entire day in this tableau, Asa demanded, "What are you doing here?"

Wenda let go of the stone just long enough to effectively shush her with an open palm.

That rankled. Well, she wasn't waiting any longer; there were more important things to do than grow old on this windswept bluff watching an addled crone engage in some sort of raven speak. The blue cloak gave a rustling sigh as she started off, and it occurred to her that maybe Wenda had followed her to get her cloak back. Of course, that was it, and so she began unfastening it, though somewhat unwillingly.

"No, no, no!" Wenda cried, flapping her hands. "You are the one who must wear it now."

Asa let the elegant brooch fastener click back into place. "Why?"

Wenda was busy searching the clearing. "Where's that horse of yours?"

"I don't know; I'm looking for him."

The woman had only to turn her eye on her two ravens and nod, and they lifted off the branch. Ignoring Asa, she took her time digging through her leather satchel.

"My mother's dead." The words sounded accusatory somehow, even to Asa's ears, yet Wenda, now crouched over her open pouch and apparently oblivious to them, continued digging. That irritated Asa. In a louder voice she repeated, "My mother's dead." And announcing it atop this mountain and having the breeze strip the words from her lips made the loss freshly painful.

Wenda lifted her head. "I know, Asa." Compassion filled her

voice though a sense of urgency overran it. She glanced toward the birch trees. "I've always known."

She returned to searching through her pouch, pushing its contents this way and that and making the strangest chirruping noises with her tongue. "Yes, here it is! What you've been wanting since you first crossed my path!" From the depths of the pouch emerged a silver-accented strike-a-light and a blackened hand torch.

Asa opened her mouth to ask a question, but a noisy disturbance in the forest interrupted. They both turned to watch Rune and her father's two horses come crashing into the open. Ears pinned and tails switching, they trotted briskly. The two ravens swooped, zigzagging, over their backs, pestering them onward.

Wenda turned. "He's coming."

By the way in which the one gleaming blue eye fixed on her, Asa knew who "he" was. "Jorgen," she murmured.

XVIII ÁTJÁN

There was something different in the air. His nose alerted him. He thought he'd sensed it last night but hadn't been sure. This morning, though, even with the blinding fog, he was certain he marked a radical change. It felt like an intrusion. He lifted his chin and sniffed. Someone or something had visited the village in the night. An animal, perhaps? Something he could track and kill?

Wedged as he was between the partially open door and its frame, he had to twist his neck with some effort to look over his shoulder. Tora abruptly resettled herself on her pillow, feigning sleep. He snorted. She was always watching him of late, eager as a fawning puppy to be his ally. That pleased him. Perhaps he'd find a use for her after all.

A suspicious crackling echoed through the misty forest and he twisted again. Those horses. Taunting him. Could that be the intrusion? Had one of the horses ventured into the settlement during the night? He sucked in a deep breath but captured only the sea's saltiness on the back of his aching throat. What was it? What was different? He turned for one more glance about the room and, assured no one was watching, at least openly, stepped outside.

Something hard caught his toe and sent him stumbling off the stone door-slab. A calf carcass, blood-spattered and with gaping eye sockets, spun to the slab's edge and teetered. His heart jumped. Instantly he searched for signs of intruders or pranksters and, in doing so, detected a line of new footprints in the mud; they led directly from the smaller byre to the longhouse. How could that be?

With his heart pounding, he listened for movement. The mist that shrouded the thatched roofs muffled the burbling of the nearby stream. Water dripped steadily from the roof onto the door-slab, splashing the carcass's stiff limbs. But then, somewhere on the mountainside above, another crackling swelled into a brief squeal and died in a single thud. He startled. Just a dead limb falling, he assured himself, nothing more. Though it took some time for his chest to stop aching. When no further noise ensued and his breathing had eased, he tiptoed across the shallow prints in the mud. He paused at the byre's partially open door to cock an ear, then laid an eye to the crack.

Alarm yanked every fiber in his body. Someone had been *here*! This was the site of the intrusion! Cautiously he slipped inside.

How still he held himself, not even breathing, waiting for his eyes to adjust. While he waited, something pale congealed from the darkness: a long narrow form stretched on the ground. That woman! The chieftain's arrogant wife! His skin contracted, forcing the hairs on his arms to stand erect. Someone had unwrapped her . . . or she'd unwrapped herself . . . and fish—where had that come from?—filled her greedy hands. He couldn't breathe. He couldn't breathe and he couldn't think. His plans were crumbling!

No, they aren't, he scolded himself. He was letting his imagination run too freely. *Steady, now; take a deep breath. Exhale. Look at the truths and figure this out.*

So he studied her. The waxen face, that same emotionless visage he'd watched across the fire these many days, now smiled in grim triumph. But how? How had she done this? What powers did she possess that she could, in the grip of death, lift food to her mouth? His mind scrambled for a plausible answer. It was all in his imagination. It was some sort of deception. It was . . . No, it was none of these things. Sucking on his lip, he reached for the fantastic and considered it: Was she a *draugr*?

And just as he thought it, her eyelid twitched—didn't it? He swallowed hard and shifted his weight onto his toes. It couldn't be. His mind had to be playing tricks. Admittedly, during childhood his father had often spoken to him of *draugrs* and Valkyrie and sorcerers. Magical people. And in his childhood, perhaps, he'd believed. But not now. *Draugrs* didn't exist.

Or did they? Did she walk with the other dead? Did they all rise and walk the village while the clan slept, slaughtering young animals and depositing their carcasses with abandon?

And what was that over there? Footprints on the byre floor, smaller than his own. A woman's prints. His mind urged him to flee. He tried to regain control, but his palms dampened in fear, and his tightening ribs crushed his breathing.

If the woman could rise, would she come for him? He remembered her last wheezy morning and the feel of his fingers pinching her nose, his hand clamping over her mouth. Of course she would.

What would she do to him?

In his haste to back out of the byre, he tripped on his cloak and nearly fell but regained his balance enough to flail away from that horrible grin.

XIX NÍTJÁN

Blood pumped through Asa's arms. The ocean winds—astringent, cleansing—filled her chest. She recognized fear, yes, but also calm. It came clear to her that she'd been running from him in one way or another almost every day of her life. Now, oddly enough, that running seemed to have taken her full circle, sending her headlong toward him. She was ready.

Surf smashed against the rocks far below, and somewhere a seabird cried. Jorgen was an evil man. He'd tricked her father and the other men and sent them sailing into their graves. He'd tried to kill Rune. Who knew how many others he'd killed or betrayed in his own greedy quest to be clan leader? With her mother dead, only she, the chieftain's daughter, could rightfully stand in his way. Most in her clan would say she was too young—how easily she envisioned Tora's sneer—but she knew to the very marrow of her bones that she had to defy him. Her palms tingled. She would battle him if needed, with knife or sword or whatever weapon presented itself, to keep him from stealing the chieftain's role.

"Get a bridle on him," Wenda said, indicating Rune. He and the two other horses huddled together, effectively penned by the circling ravens.

"I don't have—," Asa began, but Wenda proffered a beautifully braided one from her satchel.

Rune nickered as Asa neared. The white hairs sprinkled along his cheekbones revealed his many winters, but the brown eyes gazing into her own sparkled with an impish spirit. He sensed the imminent adventure. She thumbed the deep hollows above his eyes and thought for a moment about all that they'd shared, about the innate trust they had in each other. Then she fitted the bridle around his head.

"Bring him close," Wenda said, motioning. She'd ignited the torch and held it above her head as if to light their way, though the morning was now crisp and clear, the sky a cloudless blue.

Distrust held Asa in place. "What are you going to do?"

"Prepare you," Wenda replied. She motioned again, eager.

"What does that mean?" Asa demanded, pulling Rune's head close and preparing to swing onto him in a flash.

The torch lowered. Wenda's pale eye seemed to vibrate with caged anger. "Why? Why do you continue to aggravate me? I've told you you're too young to ask so many questions!"

"If you want me to help you"—Asa was getting it now; Wenda *needed* her for some reason, she needed her help—"then you're going to have to tell me what you have planned." She stared calmly straight into the ice blue eye. It wasn't nearly as intimidating as it had once been. "If it has to do with my clan or with Jorgen, then you have to tell me."

Was that a shadow of a smile on her pursed lips? If so, it was immediately replaced by a scowl. Rune butted her shoulder, impatient, and she laid a calming hand on his neck.

Sliding her gaze to Rune, Wenda said, "Jorgen is more than he appears. And less. Though most are blind to that."

Curious but cautious, Asa led Rune a little closer and let the woman continue.

"I gave his father everything he needed, yet they both wanted something more, always something more. It seems to be that way with men."

Asa's mind galloped to catch up. Wenda spoke as if she'd known Jorgen all along, but how could that be?

She'd not be receiving any immediate answer because the old woman seemed to be spinning herself into a storm. Her breath came faster and faster and her mouth parted slightly in an animal's pant. Her tongue pulsed over ragged teeth. Her eye darted from the forest to the sky to the horses to Asa and back to the sky. Was it happenstance that a bank of billowy gray clouds suddenly disguised the sun? That the surf hushed? In the pressing quiet that settled over the bluff Asa could hear her own breathing.

"Where," Wenda finally commanded, "have you seen the cloak you're wearing?"

Asa looked down at the blue garment.

"Where?" The challenge skipped across the windy clearing. "You saw it in your mind, didn't you? This beautiful blue cloak with 'the same shadowed hue as a swallow's feathers'?"

And a hem that sparkled with blue glass and clear crystal beads created in a far-off land. Asa could hear Jorgen's hypnotic voice weaving the familiar words. She gazed at the cloak's embellishments.

"I wore it," the old woman exclaimed. "I wore it when I appeared to Jorgen's father. I heard his cries and I came to him and loved him and nurtured him." The air seemed to go out of her and her shoulders slumped. She concluded sadly, "But in the end it wasn't enough."

"I thought that was just a story. Jorgen said he'd learned the tale from his father."

"Jorgen, no doubt, learned many things from his father, but greed wasn't one of them. That was his own doing. He took what was not his own."

A chill skittered along Asa's spine.

"Now you're going to take back what is rightfully yours." Wenda brandished the torch. "Bring him—Rune, isn't it?—bring him here."

Feeling as if she was being pulled into some age-old story, feeling as if the cloak she wore was its own noose, Asa moved forward. Rune, of course, obediently walked beside her. She heard her father's horses following.

Unexpectedly, Wenda lunged and swiped the torch along the ends of Rune's heavy mane. He jumped sideways as Asa tried to blunt the attack, but the hairs had already caught fire.

"What—?" Asa slapped the coiling flames away. "What are you doing?" She shoved between the old woman and Rune, warily eyeing the torch.

"He has to be ready for battle; you both do. You saw the picture-stone."

The warrior girl. Her horse's mane had been cut short. Again that chill of blood rushing through her arms set her palms tingling. Other drawings flashed through her mind—though she couldn't remember where she'd seen them—of warriors' horses, all with their manes cut short, upright, defiant.

But none of her clan's horses had had their thick manes shortened. Her clan had always lived peacefully. The occasional wanderer who shared a meal with them told of marauders elsewhere—maybe that's how she knew—but her clan had never lifted a sword.

"Time you stopped running, Asa Coppermane."

Asa squared her shoulders.

"Time you defended what is near to your heart."

Fastening her piercing blue eye on her, Wenda boldly swiped the torch beneath Rune's mane. Hairs fizzed orange and smoked. Instantly she patted out the flames, then swiped the torch again.

Rune pranced and tried to shake his head free, but Asa, seemingly in thrall to the woman's magic, held him in place. An awful stench clouded them as handfuls of hair were singed out of existence. Freed of the weight, the remaining root hairs stood upright, and the black hairs at the center rose just past the silver ones in dramatic contrast. The years, too, fell away from the old horse.

Wenda stood back to admire her work. She pursed her lips and nodded tentative approval, then proceeded to dig through her satchel. The hand she withdrew had one index finger coated a bright, sticky blue, and pushing aside Rune's heavy forelock, she painted a colorful circle around each of his eyes. "To see the target," she pronounced.

Rune shook his head and the shortened mane rippled like wind-whipped grasses. He snorted and rubbed his face against a foreleg—slightly smudging one circle—and when he lifted it to trumpet a whinny to the world, he looked every inch the valiant battle horse. He arched his neck and made the reins vibrate with his prancing, and Asa's heart squeezed.

Even Wenda chuckled at his antics before warning, "Don't you get too full of yourselves. There's more to winning a battle than appearance, though people will see what they want to see."

XX TUTTUGU

He felt their eyes upon him as he lifted the bowl. The brownish liquid smelled awful, and at first sip the broth soured his tongue and deposited bits of grit that drifted irritatingly between his teeth and sore gums. He spat the mouthful onto the floor. "Are you cooking with dirt now, Tora?"

Thidrick and Helgi giggled and doubled over. He shot them a glare. They'd pay for their insolence.

"What about that calf I just gave you?"

Tora snatched the wooden bowl from him and dumped its contents back into the cauldron. "It's not ready. You'll have to wait along with the others. And while you're waiting you can go find our missing cow." She flung the emptied bowl at him.

"Maybe he can find some cheese, too," Ketil muttered. "He's always smelling of it."

Coward that he was, the cripple didn't dare deliver his comments eye to eye.

So the chickens were ruffling their feathers. Ever since Asa had galloped away, they'd given him a wide berth, watched him with suspicion. Well, they didn't deserve his guidance, his generosity. Here he'd supplied them with meat and received only scorn. With surging blood, he rose to his feet. "You charcoal-chewers can rot in your own pus!" Feeling for the sword at his waist, he cast a menacing glare around the room and saw his wavering power yet evidenced in their hunched shoulders and averted eyes. "I want a proper stew—with meat—ready when I return." And he stalked out the door.

Fog still eddied around the settlement's structures, and he peered through it. Where was that cow? He needed to find it, needed to know that the bloodied calf carcass deposited on the door-slab had a reasonable explanation. But a niggling suspicion whispered otherwise. Someone . . . or something . . . was taunting him. That woman? A *draugr*? Well, he'd not play the fool any longer. He'd put an end to this game.

A sudden pain in his chest caught him up short and he clutched the sword's knob, wincing and gulping for air. That made his head throb even more than it had that morning, and his fomenting anger turned his knuckles white. How dare they? How dare anyone try to thwart him? They'd not take this from him. They couldn't. By Thor, he'd *kill* the next creature that crossed his path!

For some time he stood there, his chest heaving, each forceful breath a whoosh of vapor that swirled and disappeared. The wet fog gradually slicked his hair to his forehead. It beaded on his brow and ran down his nose, cooling him. When at last the pain had eased, he sought the shelter of the forest and followed the stream uphill.

From habit, he supposed, his feet carried him off the path before he reached the nearer of the outfields, and with each step his anger dulled. How many pleasure-filled days had he passed here just watching her? That brought an echo of chest pain, and he paused for a few deep breaths before continuing. Up and over the boulders he clambered, then pushed through the tangled undergrowth beside the stream. He knew he didn't need to. Secrecy was no longer necessary. She was gone. Dead.

It still troubled him that her stiff body lay unprotected, somewhere . . . somewhere, somewhere! The harrowing images tormented him nightly. He pushed aside the low-hanging pine bough, crawled beneath it, settled on the hidden rock—its cold seeped through his buttocks—and slipped his feet into the two well-worn depressions on the exposed tree root. From this viewpoint he could observe the mud-soaked outfield and all who passed through it, though on this drab day nothing ventured forth. Only a few thin, green blades, choked by the muck, clustered in moldy patches. They were a teasing hint of summer, but would the season ever come? And would any of them see it? Already their dead outnumbered their living. And the dead, it seemed, walked about even more than the living. And ate their fill.

High above him the loud flapping of wings, then the rustling of pine boughs told of a large bird's arrival. His hunger leaped and with it came the heat of blood rushing through his veins. Was it possible to catch it?

Quork, quork.

Ugh. His lip wrinkled. It was the same sound he'd heard the evening those two ravens had dumped . . . well, he preferred not to think of that. (Though he couldn't help rubbing the back of his neck, then checking his hand.)

Time passed, and bit by bit his anger crept back. The clear stream below him gurgled and bubbled across stones and pooled behind fallen branches to spin decaying leaves. Idly he stabbed at the leaves with his sword, pushing them to the bottom and holding them there until they gave up floating. The unseen bird prattled to itself.

As cold sunlight broke through the fog, a noise across the clearing signaled the approach of something large. Expecting to see the vexatious horses, and savoring the thought of stabbing his sword into at least one of them, he looked up. The vision that emerged from the opposite forest sat him straight.

It was a horse, yes, but with a rider—and no ordinary rider, for sunlight glinted off the thousand jewels embellishing this rider's blue cloak. They winked in rhythm with the horse's steps, and he found himself gaping in astonishment.

A different hunger stirred inside him. He would have that cloak for himself and relish the taking of it. He needed to spill some blood today. His fingers closed around his sword and he held himself motionless—except for the smile teasing his lips—and let the horse and rider proceed innocently toward their deaths. His heart beat painfully fast.

But as he waited for the pair to cross the clearing, the beat slipped its rhythm and his vision swam. Snippets of stories he'd told—or heard (he was suddenly confused about that)—shot through his head. *Winter winds came howling . . . He wandered. Alone. Until one morning . . . a woman rode out of the forest. And the sun blazed.*

He rubbed his eyes and blinked. This was no common rider; it was the seer! Across the clearing, riding toward him—straight toward him as if she could magically look through the overhanging boughs and see him—was the seer of his father's stories: a beautiful woman *dressed in every shade of blue.*

The hems of both garments (his lips moved with the words he'd committed to memory, though even his clever mind had never imagined anything as beautiful) *sparkled with blue glass and clear crystal beads created in a far-off land.*

The thudding in his chest doubled. Seers appeared rarely and only to a chosen few. Had she come to interpret his dreams, to confirm his wishes? Would she proclaim him clan chieftain?

Steadily she approached, steadily and slowly. Noble. Her mount could have belonged to one of the Valkyrie, for it flaunted the distinctive chopped mane, a mane that rippled like black flames with each toss of the horse's head.

Near to trembling with excitement—he was chosen!—he pushed the bough aside and scrambled up the stream's opposite bank. He pulled himself tall. *Walk straight*, he chided. *No limping.* The seer's unwavering gaze was upon him.

But as he neared the field's middle he realized with a shudder that it was no battle horse that approached, but only that runty little dun. He'd been deceived! And the rider? He squinted, his vision still wavering.

Asa! Not dead then. Or maybe returned from the dead to torment him, to prevent him from being clan chieftain. He tightened the grip on his sword. Well—dead or alive—she wasn't going to do that. She'd had her chance. And he'd labored too many seasons now molding the clan to *his* way of thinking.

The jewels captured the sunlight, shattered its brilliance, and tossed it back into the air. The dazzling display triggered random words in his mind: *She came to this man riding on a white horse.*

That gave him pause. He was confused again because there had been a white horse once. It was not owned by a seer, however, but by a sorcerer, a witch who had bewitched his father. That horse was no more. His father was no more. And, as far as he knew, that meddlesome woman was no more.

"*What is it you seek?*" she had asked. The words played out in his mind and across his lips even as Asa rode closer and closer. He heard himself mumbling the lost man's plea: "*I seek to stop wandering. I seek to not shiver. I seek to be other than alone.*"

He remembered how the woman of the story had walked with the man so that he wouldn't be lonely and how she helped him build a house of stone and wood and turf so that he needn't wander. *Then one stormy day this man said, "I am still cold. I am still hungry. Will it always be winter?"*

And she had done nothing.

His teeth ground together. Just as Asa had done nothing—after all he'd offered her. He drew his sword.

No, he thought, slowly swaying from side to side, testing the sword's feel. She *had* done something: she'd thwarted him at every opportunity! She'd attacked him and humiliated him!

One day, while the man waited beside a stream, the woman's white horse appeared to him. "I can make you warm," it told him. "I can feed you. And I can bring summer."

Was this horse speaking to him now? The blood roared through his head such that he couldn't be certain. But he wanted summer to come. They all needed summer to come. And he'd certainly be warm in that sparkling robe. With a widening smile he pictured himself in the chieftain's seat, the regal blue robe spilling over its sides to lap at the piles of food the others would bring him. All he had to do was slay this horse and slay its meddlesome rider, Asa. He should have stopped them long ago.

The dun horse was tugging at its reins. It did appear rather fearsome with its ears pinned flat, its yellowed teeth champing on the bit. He remembered the creature savaging him in the byre. A purple bruise still marked his thigh. But look now—it was shaking its head, nodding its head. Telling him what to do.

"Take my blood," the horse said, "and scatter it on open ground. And take my bones and grind them into the dirt. And take my skin, emptied of all its worth, and mount it on a wooden frame at the edge of your new field so that all who see it will know what a gift I have given you."

Yes. He would have this horse's blood. And the girl's, too. He had been chosen.

And this man, who was a dutiful man, did as the horse instructed. He picked up his sword and in one stroke . . .

XXI TUTTUGU OK EIN

The broken sword snaked a menacing arc through the air. Rune jumped and grunted surprise as blood trickled down his shoulder. Too late Asa yanked the reins to spin him away. How was she going to defeat this crazed man? She had no battle training.

Momentum had carried Jorgen off balance, and he staggered a step before raising the sword again. Both hands clutched the hilt as he lurched toward her.

She held Rune in place until the last instant, then booted him aside, and this time the sword sliced empty air.

The old skald stumbled sideways, panting. A thatch of hair that had fallen across one eye slicked itself to his cheek, yet he didn't shake it aside. His mouth gaped and closed, fishlike. Was he ill or simply out of breath? No time to ponder the answer; here he came once more. Common sense urged her to flee, but she squashed it without hesitation. She wasn't fleeing. Not from him or anyone. Not ever again.

Doubling the reins around her fingers, she prepared to signal Rune, who was growing more and more agitated. He snorted whistling blasts and broke from his prancing to paw ragged furrows into the ground. Jorgen rushed closer, his face twisted in a clenched-jaw sneer, and just before she spun Rune away a third time, she saw that the man's eyes shone as glassy as marbles. The pupils were blown so wide and black that he seemed to not even recognize her.

"What are you doing, Jorgen?" She pulled Wenda's knife from her waist and brandished it, though it was obviously more utensil than weapon. "You're not going to hurt Rune. And you can't hurt me."

Oddly, the skald retreated. As if performing some solemn ritual, he pointed the sword to the sky, then drew it close to his face, pressing its broken blade flat against his nose. With his chest heaving and the vertical sword halving his face, he focused his dark glare on her and Rune. A silence ensued in which he spoke not a word, and only Rune's impatient snorts and swishing tail made any noise. She got the impression that some sorcerer's spell—or many bowls of ale, perhaps—held him in thrall.

Rune's temper, meanwhile, was approaching a boil. Over and over he tossed his head, trying to yank the reins from her and grab the rattling bit in his teeth. Flecks of foam spattered his neck and shoulders. She'd not seen him this unruly in years, but she well remembered how explosive he could be. If he was planning one of his berserker fits, there was no way she'd be able to stay on his back. She booted his shoulder.

In response, he bucked. Hard. Before she could grab a fistful of bristly mane he bucked again, throwing her off-balance, and in the next heartbeat he was pivoting toward Jorgen. His challenging whinny split the air.

"No!" she cried, fighting for the reins as she was flung backward. But Rune had snatched the bit; he was in control, and his powerful haunches carried them straight toward Jorgen and the jagged-tipped sword now aimed at his belly. With the violence of a battering ram, Rune knocked the man to the ground. She heard the air forced out of the skald, a pained sound echoed sickeningly by Rune's deep grunt. She felt her horse falter. Had the sword gotten him? His hindquarters shivered, and for several uneven beats his gait rocked like a storm-battered ship. But then the powerful rolling gallop returned and he was circling back. The gusts blasting through his nostrils crackled like wind-whipped sails.

Jorgen was climbing to his feet, regaining his sword, and readying himself. Rune, ears pinned flat to his head, galloped straight for him. She'd not seen such recklessness in him in all the summers and winters they'd shared. Usually—with playful exceptions—they worked as one, his back soft, his neck pliant. Now she straddled one of Thor's lightning bolts. And that bolt—fierce, frightening, direct—had no cognizance of her. Still she tugged on the reins, hoping to guide him from harm. Otherwise he was going to get himself killed, get them both killed.

They were upon Jorgen again. The sword came swinging and Rune neatly dodged it. She felt him lash out with a hind hoof as he passed, nearly unseating her; she couldn't tell if the blow landed.

Then, instead of continuing in another circle as he had before, Rune stopped abruptly. His front hooves slammed the ground and his hindquarters dropped like an anchor. But they couldn't sustain the effort, and their sickening wobble—something was definitely wrong!—and near collapse sent him reeling sideways. The accompanying groan as he righted himself described so much pain her stomach sank. He was wounded; she had to get him away from this battle that wasn't his. With both hands she pulled on one rein as hard as she could.

She might as well have tried elbowing a lightning bolt. Stubborn to the bone, Rune shook away her attempts, gathered into a gallop, and pounded toward Jorgen. The fury that consumed him raged stronger, and she felt him rising into a full rear and coming at the man with flailing hooves. Just in time she clutched another hank of mane. To keep from slipping off his back she clamped her legs and pressed her cheek close to his neck. It was like flying; for that instant she was soaring toward the clouds, leaving the ground and all its burdens behind. Amidst the blur of a tilting sky she caught a glimpse of Jorgen beneath them, his arms flung across his face, as Rune's hooves came pummeling.

That moment of euphoria, of triumph over the enemy, was immediately replaced by a panicked feeling of falling, of a great weight crumbling ever so slowly, and she—helpless—with it. As if through a nightmarish fog she felt her leg jamming the ground, her ankle twisting painfully; she fought for air as a massive amount of horseflesh smothered her. She tasted mane and mud and blood.

There was a great scrambling and slamming of limbs—hooves clacked one upon the other like stone on stone—and instinctively she tried to drag herself out of danger. Her nails clawed the grit, one knee shoved against the ground in frenzied spasms. Then, somehow, she found herself unfettered. Rune lunged to his feet.

Dazed though she was, she saw that the reins tangling his legs yanked his head low. He stumbled, his eyes rolling to white. Alarmed.

Jorgen, panting in anguished gasps, was fighting to get to his knees. He located his sword in the mud and reclaimed it, clasping it with his own two-fisted fury, and staggered toward his vulnerable attacker.

She had the knife in her hand and was lunging for him even before she realized it. Rune's scream pierced her fog, and a crystalline ray of fear and anger and love brought the knife slamming down on Jorgen's back. The point tore through the wool cloak and thunked into his shoulder. A dark stain surged as Jorgen yelped.

He struggled to turn around, to face her, but wouldn't let go of the sword buried in Rune's groin. Blood splattered the black-stockinged dun legs, the mud, the cloak. She yanked the knife free and sank it into him again. Over and over she stabbed, and then he was out from underneath her and, with one arm hanging limply from his shoulder, he charged. Haphazardly he slashed at her legs. Behind him, Rune staggered sideways and fell partway to the ground, splayed in an ungainly stance.

Back and forth, back and forth, the sword swept knee-level from the ground. Jorgen lurched behind it, his haggard face twisted in a hungry, evil-eyed grin. Her blood rose up to meet his. She took a firm grip on the knife and nimbly evaded the sword's arc while searching for an opening. Her breathing roared in her ears, burned through her nostrils. She was filled with fire. The sea wind scoured her skin; the mountain buttressed her bones. She, Asa Coppermane, was the clan's chieftain, and she was going to rid them all of this menace.

From the corner of her eye she saw Rune regain his feet. The rein had broken, and one short end and a long one dangled from the bit. Although he limped, another quick glance proved his unflagging defiance; she saw it in his eyes. The sword came closer. She jumped; Jorgen chuckled. Now Rune was watching them. While his muddy mane stood erect, his forelock snarled in a mass of black storm clouds. He shook his head and snorted. Though he held his blood-covered hind leg gingerly suspended, Rune eyed Jorgen and started for him. He forced his hobbling legs to his will and lunged, running Jorgen down a third time. She barely made it out of the way of the horse's fury. He slowed to a stop, turned, and purposefully galloped over the skald, landing some near-fatal footfalls. Jorgen moaned and doubled, clutching his stomach. The sword fell free. Rune returned. She saw with horror how badly he was bleeding from his underbelly. But he tossed his head, the black forelock shooting up like flames, and managed somehow to lift himself off the ground. Not as high as before, but high enough to bring his hooves slamming down upon Jorgen's body. He lifted again and again, as methodical as a hammer, pounding the man into the mud. Jorgen's groans ended, and when she finally grabbed the broken rein and pulled Rune off him, the skald lay grotesquely twisted and silent.

XXII
TUTTUGU OK TVEIR

He was dead. Jorgen, the man she'd hated and feared, was dead. The battered face chewing mud would no longer grin at her, was in fact already hardening into some useless relic. Yet serial images of his ashen face invaded her mind: the hungry manner in which he'd always watched her, the way his eyes roved from bench to rafter and back to her when conjuring his stories, his rancid breath filming her skin, his maniacal fury as he'd slashed at Rune's neck. For every one of her fourteen summers and winters, it seemed, he'd been a thorn to her. And while the prick under her ribs had been removed, the wound throbbed hot.

Her chest heaved. She felt distinctly different; she *was* different. Blood pulsed through her veins, strong and eager. Was this how the warrior felt—keenly alive and ready for the next kill? Did one kill beget another and then another? She felt linked to the world; her heightened senses tasted the sea, inhaled the wind, fingered the mud's grit. Everything around her roared, and she felt strangely calm, master of it all.

Rune was still breathing hard, too, his nostrils fluttering dark and moist. He sidled impatiently, but his injuries finally held him in place. He cocked his hind leg, the one slick with blood, and gingerly touched the toe of his hoof to the ground. When he looked at her, he sighed. Newly worried, she peered under his belly. The tender hide gaped, revealing ragged pink flesh and strands of white gristle, all of it awash in blood. But no entrails dangled. If she could pack the wound with something absorbent—maybe some moss from the stream—and somehow coax his spirit back, he'd live. He had to. He was Rune.

She laid a hand on his forehead, found it damp and matted with sweat, and momentarily doubted her bravado. "Wait for me, Rune," she urged, and set off for the stream. Her twisted ankle buckled at once, and to her aggravation she had to make her way at an old woman's totter to the edge of the clearing. Nor was it easy to traverse the rocky banks, and her imbalance at one point sent her leg plunging into the icy current. She yanked it out with a gasp, spied some moss upstream, and clambered with more care. As she was peeling the newest, greenest moss from the rock, a raven alit in a bare-limbed ash behind her and proceeded to report her every movement with shrieking calls.

She wasn't surprised, then, to see Wenda standing beside Rune, examining his injuries, as she returned. What did shock her, though, was viewing her four-legged, lifelong friend from afar. His emaciated silhouette was a jarring outline of thin neck, bony withers, and jutting hip, truly no more than hide covering bone. His bristled mane looked ridiculous now. How had he managed, with the weight of all his winters, to become a warrior's horse for her? He'd battled for her life; he'd *saved* her life.

"Good girl," Wenda said when she saw the fistfuls of dripping moss. She squeezed the water from it and the two of them carefully packed the wound. Rune's head lifted and his eyes glistened with pain, but other than one involuntary grunt, he didn't protest.

Wenda stared at Jorgen's body, her one eye blinking in contemplation, and perhaps distrust, as if she half-expected him to rise. The wind riffled the dead skald's hair, lifted the hem of his tunic. Abruptly Wenda booted the ground, sending a splatter of mud onto his face. It freckled his nose, where a trickle of blood wormed earthward. The two ravens descended, eager to take part in the carnage. One clawed the mangled shoulder where, in a show of triumph, he ruffled his neck feathers, snapped his beak, and voiced a series of deep *kr-u-ucks*. The other boldly skipped close to the smashed face to peck at a sightless eyeball. Jealous, the first bird joined him, and in moments both eyes dissolved into bloody hollows.

"He was always blind," Wenda muttered. "So focused on his greed that he couldn't see." With a jerk of her chin she sent a wad of spittle arcing through the air. It fell short, foaming in a tiny pool within reach of his fingers. As she watched her ravens, Wenda worked her jaw, pursing and unpursing her lips, gnawing at something on her mind. "That man," she said at last, "reached beyond his grasp."

The accusatory words, though aimed at Jorgen, grazed Asa. Certainly she'd extended her reach too. Was she next to be punished? "What's wrong with reaching?"

Wenda shot her a stabbing glare. "Jorgen used *lies* to extend his reach. He threaded his stories with falsehood and with malice, and what he wove was intended only to serve his own vanity." The bitterness in her voice soured the very air around them. "He reached for something he didn't deserve. And when anyone tried to knock away his hand, he turned that hand and choked the life out of that person—or animal, as the case often was. But he had no authority to murder. He was not a god."

"Nor am I," Asa mused, mostly to herself. "But I've killed now." Something in her stomach dislodged as she watched the ravens savage Jorgen's face.

"Yes, well, that was different."

"How?"

"Eh?"

"*How* was it different? How does one killing earn applause and another death? I'd like to know."

The lone eye appraised her with some indignation, then lingered, softening. "Jorgen would have gone on killing; he's spent his lifetime killing." The wrinkly eyelid blinked. And blinked again. Moisture seemed to glisten along the spare white lashes. "In his greedy, grasping, lascivious pursuit," she continued, "he nearly took what is rightfully yours. Years ago he did take what was mine." She sucked in a sudden breath, seeming almost to tremble with a rush of anger. "He took my soul's companion, Asa, the man who was heart to my heart." She thrust her face skyward, closing her eye to the sun's glare, and gathered herself. The ravens left off their gobbling to watch.

Asa was expecting more, but in the next instant Wenda was busying herself with Rune. She ran her hands along his neck and back, and gently probed his leg, now crusting with dried blood. Pausing, fingers hovered above a hock wound, she added, "And he took from me my other love: my second treasure, my horse." She was purposely keeping her face hidden, it seemed, as she went on probing. Stiffly she bent to re-examine the wound in his groin and patted the moss pack approvingly. She was certainly taking her time. Working herself up to some other announcement? "*He*"—there was a pause for emphasis as she straightened—"killed them both. But now *you*," she said, turning toward Asa, "have killed him."

A piercing look followed, one that gradually expanded into a conspiratorial grin. How eerily similar it was to Jorgen's, the one he used when he leaned close to give a compliment, all the while wrapping that compliment around a coaxing—a coaxing so subtle that no one suspected him of twisting them to his bidding, of whispering his words into their ears so he could turn them this way and that with invisible hands.

Wenda's brow rose, and the one eye slowly blinked, nay *winked*. Something in Asa's stomach lurched violently as a sickness flooded her.

So . . . she'd been nothing more than a game piece in some longstanding dispute. Half-wit that she was, she'd allowed herself to be carefully dressed—beauteously dressed, even—and pushed into battle just as easily as her father had been pushed out to sea. To his death.

Had her own life been gambled for Wenda's vengeance? The sick feeling ate through her; she shook, caught up in the web of a violent chill. And what about Rune? She considered her selfless companion. Had the woman gambled Rune's life as well? He'd given everything for her when she'd not even asked. Her own anger surged. "So this was all your doing," she managed to say between teeth she clenched to keep from chattering. "You sent me . . . us . . . to do *your* work."

Wenda threw back her head and laughed. "*Whose* work was it to battle him?"

A biting comeback crossed Asa's tongue, but she choked it down. Confusion muddied her mind. Whose work was it, indeed? Hadn't she always known she'd someday have to confront Jorgen? Surely she couldn't sidestep him forever, lingering in the byre, dawdling at her chores. But she'd never envisioned killing him.

Her eyes spotted the knife on the ground, its blade a darkened red. She didn't remember dropping it. Well, it belonged to Wenda—in more ways than one—and so she bent to pick it up and hand it over. "This is yours." And she glared straight into the ice-blue eye.

Wenda waved it away with an annoying nonchalance. "You're not done with it, I suspect. It's no weapon, anyway, so keep it."

Asa was left standing, filled with twisted feelings of anger, self-doubt, and resentful curiosity.

As if she could hear Asa's very thoughts, Wenda said, "He was an evil man. Evil to his marrow." Asa remained stubbornly silent. "He tried to kill your horse, too, remember? And more than once. He *did* kill mine."

"I . . . I didn't know that you'd had a horse," Asa stammered at last.

Wenda laid a gnarled hand on Rune's withers and moved her stroking fingers in small circles. Her gaze clouded as she revisited fond memories. "I did. A white mare, as white as goose down and with a mane just as soft, and I loved her. One of the finest creatures I've ever known. She would have done anything for me—anything at all. And I for her."

A bold image of Rune, dreadfully wounded yet pummeling the skald with his hooves, brought a nod of understanding. "He"—she indicated Jorgen, unable to speak his name—"often mentioned a white horse in his stories. In the last wandering man story he told, a white horse ordered the man to kill him. None of us had heard that one before, and I didn't like it. Was he talking about your horse? Was *Jorgen* the wandering man?"

Wenda spoke from some distant reverie. "I haven't heard Jorgen's stories, only his father's. But I wonder if he had his father's magical skills—could he spin the stars from the skies and set them to dancing among the smoke-clouded rafters?" A honeyed smile lit her face. "That man, he could sing the fish out of the sea. He could sit at my hearth, and just by opening his hands"—and at this she parted her cupped hands and turned them palms up—"fill the room with the delicious fragrance of summer tansy, even with a winter storm gnashing its teeth at the door." Her memories overtook her then, and she fell silent. She returned to the moment with a decisive snort. "No, the man in the story—no matter what Jorgen said—was not himself but his father, a man I cared for more than any other." Nodding to the north, she said, "We kept a house beyond the next fjord after his wife, Jorgen's mother, died. For some of the year he lived with your clan and for some of the year he lived with me. We were, for the most part, happy."

"I never heard any of this."

"It was before your time, long before your time." Wenda shrugged. "Many didn't approve."

In the slanting glow of the afternoon light, they both found themselves staring at the skald and the ravens' diligent mutilation of him. Asa's mind was churning, trying to sift the truth from the tales. She didn't completely trust Wenda, never would. Finally she focused on the introduction common to all of his stories. "Jorgen always said that the wandering man in his stories wasn't happy. He said the man was searching for something but didn't know what."

"Now that does sound like Jorgen," Wenda replied. "He always breathed unhappiness and poison—though he did so through grinning teeth—at most everyone around him: his father, me, your father. His mother died when he was still a boy, you know, and better that she had, for no mother should have to claim a son such as him. It was the poison that ran swift inside him that managed to kill her, I think, and later did kill his father."

That wasn't true. "No, his father died chopping down a tree. It was an accident. My own father told me that."

The old woman glowered and Asa drew back. "It was no accident. A tree fell on him, crushing his leg. But that didn't kill him; Jorgen did. He found his father, my lifelong beloved, trapped under that tree, helpless and at anyone's mercy, and he walked away without a word. Jorgen left his father to die."

"How do you know that?"

"Because I also found him." Wenda's face clouded with dark memories. "It was late in the winter—very late—and, while we'd had some mild weather, the cold yet clung so stubbornly. The most fitful wind had been blowing all morning—I'd urged him not to go—and when all of a sudden it stopped, I knew something was wrong. I knew it at once; I could sense it. It was that dead calm that makes even the buck lift his head and hold his breath, and so I sent out Flap and Fancy to search for him while I followed on foot." She gazed into the horizon, her mind traveling backward. "He was taking his last breaths when I reached his side, in more pain than any human could bear." Vestiges of that pain contorted her voice. "For all my talents I couldn't save him, though I tried everything. I begged him not to leave me, begged him and cried. Ach! How I cried. But he was too thoroughly crushed, in body and in spirit also, because his own son had refused to help him."

A shiver rattled through Asa, punching prickles in her skin. If Wenda was right, all those years they'd been living cheek by jowl with a murderer—and not only that, the worst kind of murderer, someone who could willfully turn his back on that most sacred of blood ties. She gazed upon the skald's bloodied and mud-splattered face with new disdain.

"I'm sorry," she murmured.

Wenda shrugged, feigning dispassion. "It was a long time ago."

A meditative silence embraced them. The cool breeze stirred the needled branches of the pine trees; the ravens' gluttony created small tearing sounds. Asa's thoughts kept returning to the white mare. She hated to ask it, but couldn't stop herself. "How . . . ," she ventured hesitatingly, "why . . . did he kill your horse?"

"Because I was what he was not; I had what he'd never have." A vague smile crossed the woman's lips.

Asa waited for more, but Wenda just stared at her birds, working her lips again, and . . . was she humming now?

Rune stood with the other two horses, his head drooping, his badly injured leg hitched and balanced on the toe of his hoof. Asa walked over and laid a hand on his sweaty neck, steaming in the cold air. His nostrils still fluttered with his rapid breathing. Mourning the bloody gashes to his shoulder and chest, she slipped off the bridle. The fight had cost him so much.

She returned the bridle to Wenda, who took it wordlessly and stuffed it in her satchel. Then Asa unfastened the blue cloak, folded it, and handed it over as well. The one eye fastened upon Asa, blinking enigmatically. Was the woman waiting for something more? Expecting something else? Time passed, and then Wenda smiled—a little—and bowed her head, just slightly. Her version of a thank-you, subtly shaded with arrogance. Then she turned and, in her birdlike manner, stalked uphill toward the forest. The ravens flapped lazily around her head like summer's thunderclouds.

XXIII TUTTUGU OK ÞRÍR

"Asa!"

"We thought you were dead!"

"Jorgen said a bear . . ."

The members of her dwindling clan surrounded her with astonished but happy faces.

Dusk was falling by the time she'd settled Rune and the other two horses in an outfield—at least they could search for nibblings there—and then she'd heard a familiar bawling. She had climbed wearily through the mountainside brush to find the wayward cow and her calf, and this time she had managed to coax them back into the safety of the byre. So stars glittered in the night sky by the time she'd approached the longhouse with hesitant steps. What would they say about her unexplained absence? What tales had Jorgen spun? Would they mark her a murderer?

But here they were, welcoming her return with eager hands: hands that lifted the bags from her shoulders, hands that guided her toward the fire, hands—Pyri's stubby-fingered ones specifically—offering up a lukewarm bowl of half-consumed veal stew. So they'd found the calf.

Well, nearly everyone was welcoming. She felt Tora's critical stare even before she saw the slitted green eyes.

"Where have you been all this time?" Ketil asked as they seated themselves around the fire.

She had to withhold her answer because everyone was watching Gunnvor hurriedly shoo little Engli aside and lift the mattress that had belonged to Asa off his smaller, thinner one. Flushing, and with her chin pinned to her chest, she returned the mattress, at the same time mouthing an apology.

Of course Asa nodded acceptance. But that carried her attention to the spot where her mother's mattress had last lain (she suspected it had been burned, as was the custom), a spot now half-covered with Tora's extra-wide one. How quickly one's place in the world could change. Breathing one moment, dead the next. Stretched beside a fire one night and sprawled in the mud by the middle of the following day. Gunnvor sensed her thoughts. "Your mother . . . ," she began gently, placing a hand on her shoulder, "is no longer with us."

The words needled fresh hurt but, aware that all the faces had returned to hers, Asa allowed herself nothing more than another nod of acknowledgment and a solemn blink. She would remain emotionless, strong. As the stew held no more appeal, though, she lowered the bowl to the floor. Her obedient hands did not tremble.

"She's in the byre with the others," Ketil added, "and well seen to. Gunnvor and Astrid made the preparations—"

"We used the madder-red blanket," Astrid interrupted, "and her favorite brooch, the one with the two beasts—"

"—and Jorgen and I carried her out," Ketil concluded. "You can have a look if you want."

"No!" Thidrick protested. "Jorgen says no one can go in that byre. He says there's *draugrs*."

"Well, Jorgen's not here, is he?" scolded his mother, Gunnvor. And then to Asa, "Missing since morning. We have no idea what might have happened to him."

But no one had touched *his* mattress. They expected his return. Should she tell them?

"It's the sickness that's finally got to him," Tora jeered. Around her fingers she was winding and unwinding a short string of yarn. "It's put worms in his skull. You've all seen how he's been acting." She scanned the room for agreement. "He thinks we're putting dirt in the soup, and he's been rambling on about some ravens laughing at him and *draugrs* stalking him and—what was he saying yesterday?—something about having to wrestle the dead for smelly cheeses."

Cheeses—food! She had more food to share! "I forgot," Asa said, reaching for the bags Wenda had given her. "I have some food here." A ripple of hopeful gasps ran through the small group. She pulled out the unspoiled remnants from Jorgen's cache, the nuts and barley, then dragged out the weighty mutton loin and held it up. "This will take some time to boil—"

Clapping hands and excited chatter nearly drowned Thidrick's enthusiastic voice. "It's been months since we've had this much meat! First veal today and now mutton tomorrow. I'll fetch the water right now because my belly's getting used to this." He jumped to his feet and rubbed his stomach to everyone's laughter, then pointed at Helgi. "You get that fire stirred to a bone-cracking blaze before I get back, promise?" And he was through the door with a gush of wind and an energetic *bang*.

Asa reached for the other bag.

"Where did you get that?" Gunnvor asked, pointing. "It looks like—"

"It certainly does," said Tora. She leaned in.

"There's some fish here too," Asa announced, frowning. What was so interesting about this bag? It was what was inside that mattered. "Can you pass me a bowl?" She began pulling out flaky shards of dried fish and plopping the broken pieces into the shallow bowl, which she then passed.

Tora, meanwhile, had eased the empty bag onto her own lap and, along with Gunnvor, was studying its woven design. As Asa licked the oil from her fingers and watched the fish disappear, she thought she heard the name "Wenda" arise from the whispered discussion between the two women. That prickled her skin momentarily, though not long enough to repel the unexpected wave of exhaustion that washed over her. Warmth oozed into her hands and her face and across her chest. Her vision blurred, and the sparks that shot from the fire became pulsing orange stars that floated in a smoky sky. She felt her head begin to nod. It sagged again and again, a weight too unmanageably heavy for her ropy neck, and she fought futilely to keep it upright. As the contented chatter surged and faded, her eyelids fluttered, and she found herself swimming between two worlds, one day and one night, one real and one dreamed. Had she and Rune really battled Jorgen and won? She remembered stabbing him until he'd collapsed, and that's when Rune had . . . but where was the triumph, the invigorating sensation of blood pounding through her, the notion of invincibility? Gone now.

She shook herself awake and gave a sigh. She felt drained, utterly drained and empty and nothing more. And as she gazed bleary-eyed at Jorgen's mattress, lying empty in the shadowy corner from which he'd concocted so much fear, she questioned if it had been someone else who'd shown such bravery.

Sleepily, she watched the others talking and eating, their drawn faces lit by the fire's glow and the food she'd supplied. The longhouse felt safer than it had for many seasons. It was sparser, yes, and missing many, many faces, but ever so much safer.

"There's blood on your neck." Pyri's high-pitched voice, always overloud, drew Gunnvor's attention.

"So there is. Asa, are you injured? Asa?"

In the same instant that her head snapped back and her eyes shot open, she reached for her neck. Motherly Gunnvor scooted over for a closer look.

"Where did you come by that knife?" Ketil's voice pierced her fog.

She shook herself awake once more, dully realizing that her cloak must have swung open. While Gunnvor probed the neck wound, discovering as well her bruised cheek and still-swollen lips, Asa fumbled for and found the knife. She held it off to one side. It seemed that she'd never even seen it before. Was it the one she'd used? Yes, blood still stained the blade. But the cold metal felt abhorrent to her now, and without answering Ketil's question, she tossed it, clattering, in his direction. Gunnvor was saying something about an onion poultice, which she'd make come morning.

Thidrick returned just then, lugging two splashing pails. One after the other he dumped them into a large kettle while Helgi continued to encourage the flames. "Was it a very large bear?" he asked over his shoulder.

"What?" She pinched herself to attention.

"The bear that chased you off. Jorgen told us about it."

"No, there wasn't a bear."

Heads turned in unison. Now she was awake.

"Then what happened to you?" Ketil asked.

"Where, exactly, have you been?" demanded Tora, holding up the bag. "And in whose company?"

Now that the food was consumed, it seemed, suspicion prodded new appetites. How much should she tell?

And in even considering that question she felt herself nose to nose with Jorgen in the mud. "I . . . I left to search for food," she stammered. That was the truth, wasn't it? That is what she'd done.

"But you left in the middle of the night," Tora said, deliberate accusation in her voice.

The middle of the night. Is that when she'd left? Oh, yes. She'd awakened to find Jorgen gone and had battled him that first time in the byre. The silvery image of his knife came slashing through her mind. She relived the bone-jarring thud of being knocked to the byre floor and, strangely enough, hard on that memory came the *whump* of Wenda forcing her to the ground outside her cave. Was everyone a threat? Covetously, she eyed the knife Ketil now held; he was running his thumb along the short blade while watching her.

"I awoke to check on the horses—"

"They're up in the forest," Thidrick said. "Jorgen's been trying to get them back into the byre for days, but they won't come."

"You'll get them back," Helgi stated with a confident grin.

"They are back," she said. "They're in the far outfield. I found them on the way home." A truth, a half-truth? The muddy current in which she floundered grew stickier.

Tora pressed her attack. "So what happened after you checked on the horses?"

It had all been Jorgen's doing, her galloping away. She should tell them. Tell them that they'd been living with a murderer. Cheek by jowl. A liar, a hoarder, a murderer. *Just tell them.*

And then tell them what happened to him. Admit that she, too, was a murderer.

"I decided to ride out on Rune looking for food."

"Why in the dark?" Gunnvor asked, poking through the bowl that now contained only shreds of tails and fins and feathery fish bones sucked clean.

"The moon was bright. And there was daylight soon enough."

"Then why do you suppose Jorgen told us you'd been carried off by a bear?" Astrid mused.

"He said he tried to save you from it." In his innocent curiosity even Thidrick sounded incriminating. "He had scratches all over his face."

Her fingertips tingled and her nails got a greasy, dirty feeling.

"We saw the scratches," Tora said, "each and every one of us. And he had a badly injured shoulder, too. He couldn't lift his arm to his head."

Adopting her stern but motherly voice, Gunnvor asked, "Just what happened to you, Asa, before you rode off that night, leaving us all to worry, leaving your mother to grieve and to die alone? You must tell us."

One by one she looked into their faces: hungry, suspicious, leaderless. So eager to accuse. She squared her shoulders and accepted the blame for their worry. And she put off telling them about Jorgen's evildoings. There would be a time for that. But he was no longer a threat. He couldn't force her to act rashly. Nor could they.

"I rode out looking for food," she repeated. And the way she said it made Astrid sit back on her mattress. The young woman gathered Pyri onto her lap and listened. "Yes, it was still dark when I began," she admitted, "but I couldn't sleep and so I rode northward along the coast. I went around each of the next three fingers of land until I got to a steep-sided fjord where I couldn't go any farther. At least, I couldn't see a way to go any farther."

Gunnvor let the woven sack rest on her knee. Helgi paused from his fire play. Only Tora kept her eyes narrowed, her arms crossed.

"That's where I met the strangest woman," she continued, "a woman who'd seen so many winters she had snow-white hair. And . . . only one eye."

At that Gunnvor slid a knowing glance toward Tora.

"You don't have to believe me, of course," she said, "but I'm telling you the truth. And this woman kept two tame ravens that she talked to . . . and they talked back. Well, not in human words," she explained, "but in some sort of raven speak that this woman could understand."

Even sickly little Engli lifted his head, his mouth widening to an O and his watery eyes dancing.

"What did this one-eyed woman call herself?" Gunnvor questioned.

"Wenda."

The mysterious exchanges between Tora and Gunnvor now included Ketil. He looked at the knife in his hand and passed it back to Asa.

"She led me up to her cave by way of a path that I'd not seen before. Rune nearly fell off the cliff, but one of the ravens helped him. Inside the cave were . . . well, it was a collection of flotsam and jetsam unlike anything I've ever seen, something you might find in a giant raven's nest: fishing nets and baskets and antlers . . . hides and bones and . . . all sorts of colorful stones and shells. I don't think the place had ever been swept!"

But mushrooming doubt had infiltrated their attention. The youngsters still listened, jaws slack, enraptured, but the adults had pursed their lips, withholding approval. Something had changed.

"She sent me home with this food," she added hastily, "the mutton and the fish. Well, actually she sent me home with . . ."

"A lot more" is what she wanted to say, but where to go with that part of the story? How could she describe an old woman tossing food into the sea for the purpose of coaxing an imagined whale onto the shore?

Instead she concluded, "She sent me home with a good portion of what she had to share." Truthful enough. "And as soon as that mutton is boiled we'll have the first filling meal we've had in a long, long time."

Tora peered into the kettle. "The second," she countered. "Jorgen brought us a dead calf this morning, though he didn't say how he came by it. Did you know the cow's wandered off?"

"I found her nearby," Asa replied. "She's back in the byre. With a healthy calf."

"Oh, that's good," Astrid said, smiling. "She must have

birthed two and one died. We'll go have a look at her tomorrow, won't we, Pyri?" The little girl on her lap nodded sleepily.

"Well, the mutton's not all that much," Tora grumbled, "but it'll hold us a couple of days if I stretch some of the ends with broth. Anyway, now that the storms have passed the men should be returning home—what has it been, three . . . four days?" Ketil held up four fingers. "They've surely caught a lot of fish by now. And maybe Jorgen's off uncovering some more nuts." She looked pointedly at Asa. "He shared the hazelnuts he found when he was chasing after you."

Asa bristled. More likely Jorgen "found" those hazelnuts in his secret cache of food. How dare Tora praise him! She should tell them.

No. Not yet. Arguments and accusations would only worsen their critical situation. They needed to combine their efforts and find more food. Tora was right about one thing: The mutton would hold them only another day or two. No matter what anyone hoped, it was foolish to believe that the men had survived such severe storms and would return. They were on their own now. The nine of them were completely on their own. She had to help them realize that, and help them survive.

XXIV

TUTTUGU OK FJÓRIR

At first light Asa slipped outside the longhouse and began climbing. Though she'd been up much of the night sharing her adventure and had finally collapsed onto her mattress like a bundle of clothing, she hadn't been able to sleep soundly for thinking about Wenda. Based on the looks exchanged between Tora, Gunnvor, and Ketil, there was more to her story. She had questions. And the woman did know how to find food. Maybe she would help them.

Since they'd parted just yesterday, Asa hoped to catch up to her. So, after releasing the cow and her calf to graze around the settlement, and checking on Rune and the other two horses in the outfield—he nickered with renewing spirit—she began retracing their steps to the mountain with the picture-stone.

The task wasn't as easy as she had thought. Fog blanketed the mountains most of the morning and she emerged onto an outlook more than once only to discover that she'd hiked in the wrong direction. Nor did she find any sign of Wenda.

As the day wore on, she made her way to the summit of a thinly forested rise and paused to catch her breath and gaze at the foam-edged coastline a dizzying distance below. Again and again the waves rushed the narrow shore and dissolved, darkening the sand in ever-widening ribbons.

The parts of the mountain that had broken away stood upright in the rhythmic surf, black sentinels against a pale sky. All about them were scattered large boulders, and in the mist they resembled huge slumping creatures, seals or whales perhaps, pointed longingly toward the sea.

She scanned the coast to the north, then swung her gaze south. No sign of ships, no hunchbacked figure pestered by black birds. She looked northward again and paused.

Something had changed. She was certain one of the large boulders had moved. But how could that be? She focused on the one spot and squinted. The ocean continued running up the beach and retreating, spattering the rocks with its spray. And, after a while, one of those rocks lifted its tail and embraced the spray, ponderously and almost imperceptibly. Her heart quickened. She looked away, feigning a study of the sea's horizon but watching out of the corner of her eye and hardly daring to breathe. For the longest time she thought she'd been mistaken. The imagined movement was just a trick of light, the play of water on stone and through shadow. But again, there it was: The ocean rushed in and the black hulk shifted ever so slightly. It wasn't a rock; it was a beached whale. Food for her clan!

Her mind went galloping with this good fortune. Her heart thumped ever more rapidly in her chest and she began pacing the cliff's edge, trying to decide what to do. Seabirds had already begun circling the air above the creature. They, too, anticipated a feast. She had to get the news to her clan as soon as possible. The rising tide could carry the whale back out to sea, or it might die on the shore and rot and then all that precious meat would be wasted. This was a magnificent gift from the gods, the key to survival. She had to tell them now!

Looking over the edge, she bit her lip. It wasn't entirely impossible, though the drop was a daunting combination of undulating slope and sheer cliffs. Her pacing carried her back to the path she'd just climbed. That was the easier way, the more sensible route. But it would take three times as long, and this was urgent. Her feet returned her to the cliff's edge. Again she peered over. She'd made such descents before. Given, she'd not done so since she was a child snatching eggs from nests, but all one had to do to begin was get on one's belly, wriggle over the edge, and drop onto that flat-topped rock below.

And even as she was thinking it, she was lowering herself onto that rock and beginning the steep descent. She moved quickly, instinctively, spotting the next foothold and leaping onto it without thinking. Agile as a goat, she sprang across an uneven column of rocks, turned, and jumped down onto a chiseled ledge. Her haste sent her teetering, and for just a moment she felt the mesmerizing pull of empty air. Her breath caught as she acknowledged the perilous height. But in the next instant she gathered herself and lunged for a hold on the cliff face and rebalanced. She took more care with her progress then, though her eagerness to share the good news with her clan moved her along faster and faster.

About twenty *fot* over, a wide dry wash, much like a stony river, cut a downward swath through the boulders. Its straight path, relatively clear, offered the tantalizing possibility of a daring but even speedier descent. She could slide down for quite some way, aiming for that big boulder on the left to catch herself, then return to clambering over rocks. Prodded by excitement, she sidestepped across the mountain face until she could squat and carefully extend her heel into the pebble-strewn wash. There was no traction, of course, and immediately the pebbles fell away and she went skidding along with them. Intuitively she made herself small, tucking her chin and trying to stay balanced. As she slid, her skirt and cloak bunched uncomfortably higher until the distant ocean became framed between her bare knees. Although it was painful and nearly useless to do so, she shoved her palms into the pebbles to slow her descent. Her heels dug shallow tracks in the damp gravel.

For a while the surge and ebb of cascading rock filled her ears. She slid so fast at times that tears came to her eyes; then she'd slow to a near stop and have to push herself onward, wobbling and skidding some more. Without marking it she knew she was rapidly covering a great deal of ground.

The boulder was rushing up to meet her now, and she leaned her weight a little to the left and thrust out her leg to catch it. But a slick patch at that very spot spun her away, and the boot that jammed into the boulder only served to flip her over and send her spinning down the slippery mountain feet-first on her belly. The pebbles grew to jagged stones that began pummeling her hips and hammering her cheek. Frantically she grabbed at one after another, but her hands only shredded on their points.

A sharp pain poked her side, eliciting a gasp, and she knew Wenda's knife was somehow twisting into her. She couldn't reach for it. She was helpless. Faster and faster it seemed she was being pulled downward, and she envisioned herself a bit of twig carried upon a mountain torrent. She was going to plummet over the next drop-off!

Her fingers touched a weedy stalk and grasped. They ripped along its length, burning, and came away empty, but that slowed her just enough that she was able to grab another stalk and hang, tight against the mountain, hearing the pebbles ping past and eventually fall away into silent air.

Helpless as a baby clinging to its mother's breast, she pressed her cheek against the mountain's gritty skin and tried to catch her breath. Fear sent uncontrollable tremors coursing through her body. The very magnitude of her situation dizzied her, and the black tide edging her vision seemed to be threatening blindness. The pounding surf became a pounding in her head, and time slowed.

Gradually, though, she quieted herself. Every last bit of her throbbed, and she took mental note of her injuries: painful welts on her head, forearms, hips, and knees; blood on her hands and, probably, her face. But nothing she wouldn't survive.

The patches of raw skin on her cheek and palms suddenly blazed to pinpricking life, and she had to blink away tears. The icy gusts from the ocean delivered no relief.

When her knees felt as though they would dependably lock into place, she slowly drew them underneath her, wincing. Cautiously she tested her foundation, then sat up. It annoyed her that she couldn't stop trembling. She brushed the hair from her eyes, combed grit from her brows, and adjusted the cloak around her shoulders. In doing so she discovered that her father's two childhood gifts—the copper spoon and the horse-headed comb—had broken off and fallen somewhere. That saddened her. She felt for the knife and realized it was missing, too, even as her wandering gaze caught its glint among the scree farther up the wash.

Was it worth retrieving? Any knife was precious, but she'd stabbed Jorgen with that one, and recalling how the iron handle had bitten her palm when its blade plunged so hungrily into his shoulder (and how much of that was her own hunger?) and then the jolt as metal met bone (she could envision the knife's bloody point scratching the white bone) sickened her. These were images she didn't want burdening her the rest of her days.

Leave it.

Leave it to the ocean winds to scrub clean. She'd have no more part in killing.

So she crabbed sideways on her hands and knees until she was safely out of the wash and onto solid rock. Pleased, she glanced up the mountainside and was impressed by the great distance she'd descended—almost halfway—and there lay the knife, the length of three bed sheets apart from her.

Foolish to leave it. It was a tool as much as a weapon. What if she needed to stab a fish or crack a nut? Her father's oft-repeated warning to think beyond the moment echoed in her mind and suddenly, maybe because she was this close to the ocean, she felt the insistence coming directly from him. Determined to prove his faith in her, she swallowed a sigh and ever so cautiously crept back onto the slippery, rock-strewn face. For every bit of progress she made climbing, she sank nearly as much, but eventually she neared the knife. More pebbles gave way and it skidded into her outstretched hand. The cold iron delivered an odd comfort.

Below her the surf roared louder, beckoning as well as taunting. The tide was rising. She could see that the whale was still there, but she couldn't tell if it was alive or not. More and more birds circled it in a screeching cloud.

She allowed a little shiver of pleasure to ripple through her. How excited everyone would be! They'd all rush to the shore—all except little Engli anyway. Tora would be lumbering behind, shouting orders, no doubt, which was fine. She herself had no memory of how that whale of two summers ago had been butchered, though she recalled standing at its leathery side and staring into its filmy brown eye wider than her two hands. But, oh, how well she remembered the *mylja*, and at that thought her tongue watered. She'd taste it again soon. And *spikihval*. And *gryn*. At last their bellies would be full. And there'd be oil for their lamps, bone for their smoothing boards, and floats for their fishing nets.

Excitement bubbled within her. Immediately she resumed her clambering. She adjusted her descent to the mountain, sometimes scooting across precarious sections on her butt and sometimes turning to face it. Then she'd pick her way almost blindly, her chest scraping the rocks, her outstretched arms suspending her weight until her toes could search out support.

She came to a very steep part, so steep that if she even paused to consider how she was going to get across it, she knew she'd freeze in fear. So before her next breath came she eased onto a crevice and kept going. Slowly now, slowly and carefully. She'd seen a sea star once, a large spiny one, clinging to a rock after a storm. That's how she felt as she pressed her body to the cliff, every pore sucking to the rock like the sea star's sticky legs. Her cheek measured every granulated imperfection as her body crept sideways. She was going to make it home.

The surf pounded in her ears, and she wanted to glance downward but couldn't risk the unbalance of craning her neck until she got through this section. So, without seeing, she extended her leg, blindly tapping the rock until she found the last little ledge. She pushed off with her other foot, leaped, and there, she'd made it.

A shallow cleft with an uneven surface and small outcroppings provided a vertical ladder of sorts, and she dropped quickly through its damp, cold shadows. Only a little more to go now. She braced against an outcropping and leaped, then crouched, sprang, and dropped further, cradling herself in a bowl between two boulders. She twisted slightly and sprang again.

A biting pain crushed her wrist. She was yanked sideways, somehow snagged. Madly she flailed her legs, trying to gain some support. Pain ate through her arm. What had happened? She kept kicking, finally found a foothold, and propped up her weight. The fire blazing along her arm erupted in searing flashes of light behind her eyes. She fought like a wild animal trying to pull her hand free, but the harsh truth was she was trapped. Somehow, it seemed, a rock had shifted as she had sprung, and its crushing weight now clamped her hand as cruelly as the wire did a hare.

Water filled her eyes and she couldn't blink it away. Panicked, she peered blearily toward the shore. The whale was still there, a hulking mass of life that could restore her clan. She'd been so close to saving them.

XXV
TUTTUGU OK FIMM

The searing pain vanished surprisingly fast. She couldn't even feel her hand. She yanked this way and that, sidling left and tugging, then lifting onto her toes and waggling. Only her skin gave the fleeting illusion of slipping. Her flesh strained, but tied as it was to sinew, which was sewn to bone, which was pinned under a great rock higher than her shoulder, she was well anchored in place. On impulse she tried shoving her hand deeper under the rock and twisting. A painful crackling shot through her wrist. Had she broken some bones? Panic flooded her. What was she going to do? How was she going to get free? Frantically she struggled, flailing and tugging at her arm, and again she envisioned a hapless rabbit kicking in its death throes.

Her chest tightened as if between great iron tongs, and that awful blackness seeped around the edges of her vision. The pain that had fled her hand burned through her arm, blazing into an excruciating scream and—had that noise really come from her?—she pummeled the rock with her fist. It didn't budge, and now her good hand was scraped raw. Collapsing awkwardly against the cliff face, dampened with sweat, she fought for air. What was she going to do?

Maybe holding very still would let her hand relax enough to slip free. Against the crushing grip of her ribs she forced a deep breath. The sea air left a much danker taste on her tongue now, and it was a relief to expel it and stand quietly. Forced by her tethered position to stand, she rested her cheek against the bluff's stony face—how deathly cold it was, and how gritty—and waited. Breathed in, breathed out, in and out, willing her hand to loosen. Below, the tide served as her guide: As it rushed to shore she inhaled and held herself still, thinking but not thinking, and as it receded she pushed out her breath and her fear and sent them away on the waves. A moment of nothingness, with only her heart fluttering as faintly and fast as a dying rabbit's, then the tide returned and she inhaled.

Needles pricked her suspended arm like a thousand bees, and when she'd waited long enough she tugged at it once, then again, yanking with all her strength, but nothing happened. She was stuck. Half-heartedly she gave another tug, then gave up.

The day stretched long. Waves became her world; their soughing filled her ears, their sparkling glazed her eyes. They numbed her to the stinging, so that eventually her arm past her elbow felt separate, as if it were someone else's limb. If she didn't look up to see that her arm was, indeed, attached to a crushed hand, she'd not even know it existed.

Would someone find her? The bitter absurdity of that elicited a snort. Would anyone even miss her? Rune would. And the thought of him living his days alone, wondering why she'd abandoned him, stabbed her.

To keep that image from her mind, she put order to the world around her. She named what few plants she could see. She counted the rocks in the distance, the ones tumbling into the sea, and mindlessly arranged them by size. The slumping silhouette that was the whale still resided among them. When she ran out of things to assess, she watched the waves splash against the rocks and marked the passage of time by the incoming tide. In and out, in and out rushed the waves, each time climbing a little higher on the shore. The water rose around the rocks and the whale. Splashing, caressing. The creature began moving more actively; its tail arched in anticipation.

No!

With indescribable sadness she watched the rising tide rock the whale from side to side, then lift and float the creature free. It hung in the shallows awhile, gyrating slowly, but the traitorous waves coaxed it out to sea. Tears blinded her to its passage. When she blinked them away, the whale was gone.

The ocean gives and the ocean takes. Isn't that what the men had always said? Well, this winter it had surely taken everything. All the fish. All the men. Her father. And now the whale.

For the longest time after that she could only stare at the empty place on the shore where the whale had been. The sun deepened to a golden orb in an iron sky and ever so slowly dipped toward the ocean. The wind lessened, the air grew chill. She shivered.

Night was falling now and she had no shelter, no way to stay warm. Pinned against this bluff, her arm strung past her head, she was helpless. That ignited a small fire, and again she struggled with unreasoning fury to free herself. She kicked and twisted and grunted and even lost her footing at one point, so that for a horrendously painful moment she was actually hanging in the dusk by her trapped hand. She shrieked as bones cracked. From far, far above came a familiar nicker, one shadowed with worry.

Frantically she scrambled to regain her feet. "Rune?" she called, not knowing exactly why. Did she expect him to fly down here and rescue her? Even he had his limits.

The darkness delivered no answer, and when the winds had swept away his name she felt very much alone. She shivered uncontrollably and yearned anew for the comfort of wrapping her legs around Rune's furry sides, of urging him into an exhilarating gallop. The beach below was murky, but she remembered how often they'd gone flying along it, spraying sand and scattering raucous gulls. How sad that she'd never ride him again. She'd never even see him again! And at that realization a great, solemn weight settled upon her.

She was going to die.

That night was the longest, and the shortest, she'd known. She stood throughout, dozing and wakening, shifting her weight from one foot to the other as her knees stiffened, her hips complained. How did horses manage it? Alternately she tucked her free arm against her chest for warmth or beneath her cheek as a cushion.

If she stood completely motionless she could cling to the small pocket of warmth created by the diminishing heat from her body. Or maybe she imagined that. The rock itself was as cold as ice.

Glittering stars poked from the black sky, fiery embers from the gods' fires. There was the Great Star and Aurvandill's Toe and Frigga's Distaff. They arced across the sky with surprising speed. And then they were winking out one by one, fading with the graying sky as a new day approached.

She must have dozed more deeply then, because when the burning pain in her suspended shoulder awoke her it was full light. Awareness of her situation crept back to her and with tentative hope she tugged at her trapped arm. Nothing had changed.

The rocky cliff saturated her with cold, sending violent shivers through her body. She ached for the sun to thaw her, but the orb that climbed into the sky that day withheld its warmth. From horizon to horizon the sky yawned a hazy, fish-belly sort of white. No clouds, no birds. Lifeless. Even the ocean languished. The waves that rolled shoreward curled upon themselves with a hushed restraint.

She cupped her free hand over her nose and mouth and blew moist air, warming her face. Her tongue felt thick and sticky, and she realized how thirsty she was. When had she last had anything to eat or drink?

Half-wit! What was the point of worrying over hunger or thirst when she was going to die? Yet her stomach panged stubbornly, even as a wave of nausea washed over her. The cold rock suddenly became comforting, and she touched her cheek to it. How much longer?

The whole of that day passed in a stupor. Now and then, when the fire stirred inside her, she maneuvered around and tugged at her arm. But each time she gave up sooner. It was getting harder to fend off the dizziness, and she had to blink purposefully and press her fingers to her creased forehead and remember to breathe.

The lackluster sun dipped once again into the ocean. But its disappearance intensified her shivering. The tremors shook her to the very core, battered her body into exhaustion so that she slumped against the bluff when she could no longer shuffle from side to side, stamping her feet to keep her blood stirring. The task was just too difficult, and she began to welcome the thought of surrendering to the cold and dying.

Sometime later—and who knew how much later, for time seemed to have lost any measuring or meaning—an insistent sound, a guttural croaking, nudged her eyes open. She blinked. It was morning again, another day. With dull appraisal she noted that her shoulder had stopped hurting; she couldn't feel it any more than her crushed hand.

A stone's throw away, perched on a rocky lip, was a raven. A little beyond and above it was another. Wenda's ravens? She craned her stiff neck as far as it would go back and squinted upward, half-expecting to see the wizened old woman climbing down. Nothing but jutting rock against a wintry blue sky. An ocean gust whipped her hair, burnishing her already taut skin and sucking the remaining moisture from her cracked lips. With a wry smirk that opened a new fissure she recalled the fish Wenda had hung outside her cave to dry. That's what she'd become: a drying fish.

The croaks of the nearer raven switched to excited chatter. Up and down it leaped on the breeze, hunching its shoulders and shaking the ruffled feathers on its head. It hopped sideways, as if in play, and returned. The other raven spread its wings and let out a yelp, after which both birds studied her intently.

She stared back, urging her mind to take action, to think. Had they come to peck out her eyes as they had Jorgen's? Well, she wasn't dead yet; they weren't having her eyes! And she lifted her arm to shield her face. That alone made her dizzy. Beneath the protective shade of her elbow she closed her eyes.

The two birds took up a gurgling, smacking, clacking conversation, and it seemed that they were talking to her—no, they were talking *about* her. Somehow, behind her eyelids, she understood their raven speak. They were telling her story. They spoke of her battle with Jorgen, of her bravery and that of her horse. Only they didn't call him by name, it was more like "four-feet thunder." They described the picture-stone that overlooked the ocean, the one with the girl warrior on horseback. They went on to recount some of the adventures she and Rune had shared, events they could not possibly have known about. No one but she and Rune knew about those.

She blinked her eyes open. These weren't Wenda's ravens after all; they were the two ravens that belonged to the great god Odin, the ones who carried to him all the secrets of the world. Of course they knew her story.

So was she dead? Had they come to take her to Valhalla? She extended her fingers along the rough cliff wall, pressing her tips into the gritty surface. It certainly felt real. She looked skyward for Odin's Valkyrie, the winged daughters who escorted the dead to the afterlife. Wispy clouds filled her view, but no otherworldly messengers.

Of course not. They came for the battlefield's dead, the fallen heroes. She wasn't a hero.

One of the ravens trilled, a nearly musical sound, while the other voiced a rhythmic drumming. Frowning, she looked more closely. Purple-black feathers, ponderous bills, shaggy beards. No, they were just two ordinary birds, come to peck out her eyes. *I traded my eye for something that I hold more dearly than life itself*, Wenda had boasted. *What will you trade for a whale?*

But there was no whale. And she closed her eyes and waited.

XXVI
TUTTUGU OK SEX

Traveling without her birds made her skittish. They served as her eyes—her good eyes, anyway, since the one eye she owned shrouded her world in a perpetual haze. How much longer before the haze gave way to night?

The forest here lay exceptionally quiet. In the distance, unseen, water cascaded noisily down the mountain; but along this needle-covered path all she heard was the squishing sound of her own feet alternating with the soft plunk of her walking stick. Trunks stood silent watch in every direction, but there was no movement among them: no animals, no birds, no life. Wenda trudged on, thinking. What had made her turn around?

Jorgen was dead. Those words never failed to bring a satisfied smile. So many years she'd lived anticipating the day. The burnt bones had foretold the girl's coming again and again, continually cautioning her to patience, and ach! it had been frustrating. Twice daily, winter and summer, she'd left her cave to look to the south, always squinting into the shadows across the fjord and seeing nothing. Even when the girl first appeared, she didn't come directly. She'd ridden away and returned and then had to be coaxed to the cave with barley cakes. And here was another question: What had caused her to bake a double batch that day? The bones hadn't indicated the horse—Rune, his name was—but she'd been happy to welcome him into the cave that was her home. Flap and Fancy had definitely not been pleased, and they'd complained with their usual mewling and bickering, but for her it was a tonic to have a horse so near again. The sight of him gave comfort; the smell of him soothed as no herb could.

She paused to catch her breath. Something about that heap of red-brown needles tucked close to the nearest trunk drew her eye and she poked through it. Jewel-green leaves, freed of the weight, unfurled along a tender stem. She smiled. Another year come. As many as she'd witnessed, the pure brilliance—the undaunted spirit—inherent in each dawning summer never failed to stir her. Yes, everything was unfolding as it should. Leaning into her stick then, she continued up the muddy path. Summer may be on the way, but at present she was cold and in need of a steaming bowl of tea. She hoped they had some brewed.

The clan, *his* beloved clan as well as Asa's, needed a skald, and though she cherished her privacy, she knew she had to reclaim his seat beside the fire. That's why she'd turned around. The people needed hope. A good skald provided hope.

High above, an errant wind disturbed the treetops. Was the weather changing? She picked up her pace though her chest strained.

They needed a good leader, too. A confident chieftain who'd

govern with a generous heart and a wise head. A leader who would put the needs of the clan above his—or her—own. Would they have one?

It irked her that she didn't know. What was the purpose of trading her eye for knowledge if she couldn't *know* everything? The apparent trickery related to her bargain sent her stick slamming into the mud with vexation. She chewed on that idea as she climbed, aware that her wheezy exhalations added fleeting puffs of mist to the forest's skirts.

Perhaps knowledge was limited to facts, to the objects she discovered in her travels, to the terse words and images delivered to her by her ravens. Perhaps humans, ultimately, were unknowable. The girl, without question, continued to surprise her, continued to reveal a depth of character that she'd never expected. As much as she probed, Asa yet remained a mystery, one who possessed a wisdom beyond her years. She would enjoy instructing her.

Up and down she trudged over the knuckles of the mountain's splayed fingers. The light filtering through the forest slowly dimmed as evening approached. She'd not yet caught the scent of smoke that would signal the settlement. Flap had assured her it wasn't much farther, but he'd miscommunicated distance on more than one occasion. He couldn't be made to understand the difference between him flying a straight line through the air and her traversing this mountainous terrain on foot.

A sodden pinecone unbalanced her and sent her tumbling to the ground with a surprised grunt. Ach, she was getting old!

Muddy debris coated both palms and soaked through to an elbow. Fuming, she planted the walking stick and climbed to her feet with some effort. How she missed clipping along these paths on horseback. With each passing year the mountains grew steeper. She gauged the distance to the next crest and heaved a sigh. That was another thing: She could see so much farther from the back of a horse. She enjoyed looking ahead. Adjusting her cloak, she proceeded.

As the path narrowed and darkness pressed in, her steps slowed. Many times she'd traveled this way as a young woman, often at night, so she could rely on memory to guide her. But no one much bigger than a fox had passed here in a while, and even when she spotted what she thought were the trail markers, she had to blink and blink again, for they, too, had aged, and that left her frowning and feeling somewhat adrift.

At last, when she emerged from the forest to overlook the fjord, she found the sky glowing under faint moonlight. The waters reflected its silvery sheen. And below, huddled on a scrap of land between the base of the mountain and the inlet, lay the dismal settlement. If not for the wisp of smoke coming from the longhouse, she'd have thought the place abandoned. The muddy fields lay barren of crops; the byres, by their silence, seemed empty of livestock.

Cautiously she made her way down the slope and crept through the dark to the longhouse. As she rapped her stick on the door she noted the short pine bough mounted above it. Someone, at least, clung to hope. "I'm a wanderer needing a roof," she called. "You know me." Within she heard murmuring and the footsteps of someone's approach. When the heavy door opened a crack, Tora's narrowed green eyes peered through. Her challenging expression retreated into reluctant recognition, and the door was pulled open to a stale and dreary winter-chilled room. Only eight dull faces met her gaze as she entered. Was that all who were left?

Tora made a small show of having to maneuver the heavy door closed all by her groaning self, then returned to the fire, pointedly not offering a seat. The woman could certainly hold a grudge.

"You've not seen me for many a winter, but you know me, as I knew Jorgen's father." Distrust showed on their ashen faces, distrust mixed with fear, especially on those of the four children. The young boy lying in his mother's lap seemed especially frightened, and she guessed that was due mostly to her empty eye socket. Well, she was not a pretty sight anymore, but the women had aged too, and she had to search from one to the next for a familiar feature. Standing shakily beside his straw mattress, one hand still gripping a half-hidden knife, was old Ketil. He recognized her.

"How is your leg, Ketil?"

"Like the wolf's got it in his teeth, Wenda." That was Ketil: always grumbling. "You're welcome to our fire."

The chieftain's seat on the far side of the hearth remained empty, as did the skald's. Best not to hesitate. She confidently picked her way among the mattresses and discarded utensils and lowered herself into the skald's place. At once a warmth unrelated to the fire oozed through her joints, offsetting the clan's unspoken disquiet. Her beloved used to sit here. Those had been such happy times. She'd help weave some more.

Casting sighs of annoyance, Tora peered into a cooking pot, stabbed a small slice of mutton, and deposited it onto a plate. To that she added a meager ladling of cooked barley and signaled for it to be passed. "We're missing some of ours," she announced. "Besides the men off to sea, there's a girl of fourteen winters, the chieftain's daughter, about as willful as the wind. She came back from some foolish venture only to pass one night and disappear again."

Tora caught her hiding a smile as she sniffed the mutton. "Yes, it's yours," Tora snapped. "And we thank you." Then she went on. "The other person we're missing is Jorgen the Younger, gone two days now. Maybe you know something?"

Best to be blunt. "Your Jorgen is dead."

"How?" Ketil asked.

"That's for later," she replied, taking command—temporarily at least. "It comes closer to the tail of the story."

A glance at the empty faces showed no reaction to the news about Jorgen. She realized that this wasn't because his death was welcomed, but because it was expected. Death had become routine to these poor people. *Any one of us could be next,* they seemed to be thinking.

So who had mounted the pine bough?

"As for Asa"—and she paused to monitor their surprise at her naming the missing girl, again stifling a smile—"she's finding her way."

She turned to Tora. The woman carried her self-anointed authority with ease—flawed by selfishness, yes, but such was her nature. Smart of Jorgen to have utilized her. "Do you have butchering knives?"

She received a perfunctory nod. "Why?"

Information, yes. Explanation, no. "Get them out, along with the whetstone. You'll need to have them sharpened."

The softly hissing fire marked time as the two stared at each other and the rest of the clan watched. It became obvious to everyone that Tora wasn't taking orders. Astrid rose. "I'll get them."

"What are we going to carve up?" Tora sneered. "The mutton's nearly gone and the storeroom's empty."

Wenda straightened her shoulders and answered in a voice that nearly boomed. "A whale."

Ketil's jaw fell open. "Have you found a beached whale then? In truth?"

"I've not found him, but you will—soon. Now get to sharpening those knives." She gestured with an insistence that set most—but not all—hands to working.

"But what about Asa?" Gunnvor asked. "What is it you know about her?"

How much should she tell? She fluttered her hands at those still idle. "And gather some baskets, too, some big ones." When she pinned her one eye on Tora and delivered its solemn, expectant blink, even that stubborn woman finally shuffled off to work.

"Now," she said, slapping her knees and working to recall the tricks of a good skald, "let me tell you a story about a girl with hair the color of copper, a girl who was no ordinary child. A young woman who came to do extraordinary things."

XXVII

TUTTUGU OK SJAU

A thin, high-pitched whine bored through Asa's torpor. She forced her eyelids, incredibly sticky and sore, open just far enough to discover the rocks teeming with tiny, winged insects. Thousands of legs and slight bodies surrounded her, all engaged in an excited dance. Confused, she blinked hard and rolled her eyes upward. The creatures were congregating around her wrist—odd that she couldn't feel them—and the underside of the dislodged boulder. They were preparing to feast on her dead hand! Instinctively she tried to pull free, but of course couldn't. How long before they gnawed their fill and doubled back, came spilling down her arm, and crawled over her and into her? With all the strength she could muster, she lifted her free arm to shoo them away. They scattered momentarily, as weightless as blown ash, and resettled. Again she waved them away. They returned. It was no use. She closed her eyes and tried not to think about them.

From somewhere in the sky behind her, a heavy *swoosh-swoosh* announced the return of the ravens. Had they been watching all this time, just waiting for her to stir? Irritated, she opened her eyes and watched them alight in their same places and immediately resume their cacophonous duet. As on the previous day, the larger bird gurgled and chattered while the smaller one shook its head with excitement and hopped sideways and back on the rocky lip. Then it flapped to a boulder below and looked up, obviously hopeful she would follow.

"I'm snagged," she managed to croak, "in case your beady eyes haven't noticed." Her scratchy throat made her sound like an old, old woman.

In a direct series of hops and winged leaps, the raven returned to her side. It found a perch so close to her face that when it parted its beak to scold with a jarring *kra-a-ck* she could see its black tongue spasm. It cocked its head and studied her with such intensity, such purpose, that she grew a little panicked. Was it preparing now to peck out her eyes? She covered her face, watching the bird from under her elbow. If it so much as leaned in her direction, she was going to grab it by the neck and bash its body against the rocks. The other bird set to shrieking at once, and with such alarm it must have understood her thoughts.

Swallowing with great difficulty, she muttered from beneath her protective elbow. "Well, if you're both so smart, why don't you fly off and find Wenda? Bring her here to help me."

The smaller bird lifted off the rock and repeated its pattern of flapping onto a lower boulder, then another and another. Near the bottom, it looked up at her.

This was ridiculous. "I can't follow you!"

Rebuffed, the bird spread its wings and flapped up the coast.

She watched its image shrink until, far in the distance, it landed on an enormous rock. Only a tiny black silhouette now, the raven amused itself by hopping from one end to the other, leaping into the air and coming down, spinning, and all the while yelling and yodeling in agitated raven speak. Unmoved, she watched the performance. The gusts picked up the strident calls, braided and unbraided the notes, and rushed the fragments across the bluffs where they teased the larger raven into response. His calls came sharp and loud, the demanding *kr-r-rucks* and *gronks* so eerily like commands that she looked up. He'd become another creature entirely: His plumage, bristling like stalks of black wheat, doubled his size, feathery horns arose from his head, and his eyes rolled to white as he bobbed and screamed like some disembodied spirit. What was happening?

Such racket seemed destined to draw birds from all over, but none appeared. And then, as if by mutual signal, the clamor ceased. The coast and Asa's tethered roost on the bluff fell extraordinarily quiet. Gooseflesh prickled her arms. This time when she looked up, the raven was casually preening its feathers, now folded smooth. It lifted a claw to scratch its cheek, then paused to calmly return her stare. The wind whipped through her hair, the ocean tide surged in and out, and the day stretched on.

Until a percussive sound like metal upon metal came from far up the beach. The monotonous hammering arrived as regularly as her heartbeat. The nearer raven listened with keen interest. It didn't seem possible for a bird to make such a noise, but it was indeed the raven up the coast calling in a rhythmic monotone. The annoying *ping-ping-ping* pounded in Asa's skull until she thought she'd scream. Every fiber in her being wished to boot that bird off its rock, and she shook her fist in its direction. Just then the rock, as if performing her will, jerked with such force that the raven flapped into the air. It circled and landed. The rock writhed, flinging the bird again, and the fog vanished from her head. It wasn't a rock; it was the whale! The whale had returned!

Summoned from memory, happy cries drifted down the beach as they had two summers ago, when her clan had discovered that other beached whale. The men—including her father—had carried their sharpened knives high, laughing and boasting of the ferocity of their blades. The boys had competed in carrying woven baskets heavy with meat back to the longhouse. Her mother—and at that a familiar musty fragrance, achingly comforting, tickled her nose—her mother and the other women had scurried to bring pots of water to a boil, to scoop out salt and unwrap spices. Astrid had attacked the storeroom, sweeping with such vigor she'd not even noticed the clumps of fallen turf settled atop her head scarf.

The imaginary laughter faded as the murmuring waves reclaimed their beach. How long had it been since she'd heard that sort of laughter among her clan? This winter had been so harsh, first with the endless rains and then the unceasing cold and the sickness. They needed this whale; they needed the sustenance it could provide, and they needed the hope it would bring. She had to tell them.

Only she couldn't. Her crushed hand, anchored to the useless rope that was her arm, had her securely attached to this cliff.

She needed to cut that rope.

Stop. Cut off her hand? Could she even manage such a feat? How much would it hurt? And how would she ever ride Rune? No, it would be too painful, and she'd be left a cripple, a charcoal-chewer sitting beside the hearth, unable to contribute to the clan's needs, and thus despised. She just had to wait a little longer. Someone could yet find her.

But how much longer would the whale remain? It had vanished once. The next tide could float it away. Or worse, it could die and rot on the shore, a horrendous waste. And she'd die in eyesight of it, a rotting waste herself. No, she'd not even be in sight of it, because these cursed birds would have her eyes pecked out before she took her last breath!

She gave the near one a good glare. Her breath was coming fast now, balanced as she was at the precipice of something very big, something frightening. If she spent any time at all thinking about it, the fear would overtake her and she'd never edge this close again.

She pulled out Wenda's knife and tentatively drew it across her arm, as close to the wrist as possible. Nothing but a pink line. She pressed harder and this time brought forth a sliver of bright red along with a gasp. The pain was too much! And with a blade so dull she'd barely get through flesh, never mind bone. Furious, she hammered the knife's butt against her forearm.

That reminded her of stabbing Jorgen. Her stomach twisted, as it did each time she reconjured the shock of plunging the knife point into him, of feeling the jolt as blade struck human bone.

She needed another tool. Quelling her stomach's distress, she cast around for a rock, a sharp one, within her limited reach. Spying a possibility, she snatched it up and brought it down hard on her wrist. Nifelhel, that hurt! Again and again she slammed it into her wrist, and the pain fired along her arm and ravaged her shoulder. She refused to acknowledge it. It wasn't her own arm she was attacking; it was a torturous binding, a stubborn rope that had her trapped on this cliff when she needed to be leading her clan to the whale.

While she labored she became aware that the other raven had returned. They were both watching her, though she didn't pause to look up. This wasn't their concern.

For some reason the muffled thuds lured Wenda's words from memory and sent them circling through her mind. *You want a whale? What would you trade for it?* The words faded in and out, grew strong, and solidified into a chant, urging her to greater effort. *What would you trade for it? What would you trade for it?* Methodically she pounded. Something cracked, a bone hopefully, and blood trickled down her elbow. She kept smashing, moving as if in a hypnotic dream, not thinking, not questioning.

It won't cost you an eye, but rescuing your clan may demand something equally dear.

Her wrist was a bloody mess, but far from broken. The rock

wasn't going to be enough. It wasn't big enough; she wasn't strong enough. *What would you trade? What would you trade?* The chant prodded her to a frenzy. She had to think of something; she couldn't stop. If she stopped now, she'd . . . No! She wasn't stopping until she was finished.

All right, she couldn't break her arm by pounding it; she needed to snap the bones, snap them the way she broke kindling over her knee. Only she didn't have that kind of leverage. Unless . . . weighing the rock in her hand, she pondered the possibility: If she could wedge the rock under her wrist just right, use it like her pointy knee, she could maybe twist her arm with enough pull to bring it down hard and sudden across the rock, and maybe her bones would snap. Instantly she set to work.

Shoving the rock underneath her mangled wrist bloodied her good hand. She didn't bother to wipe it, just grasped her forearm, sank as low as she could, then sprang up and, as she came down, threw all her weight against her arm.

The bone snapped. She felt it at once, a clean, searing pain. Sweat beaded her brow; she could feel that, too. And the chill breeze across her parched lips. Gingerly, she felt along her arm. There was a telltale bulge, but she was still tethered to the boulder. Gritting her teeth, she crouched, sprang, and yanked. Nothing happened except that more pain surged through her body. She leaped again, and this time another bone cracked. She felt her arm sag at an unnatural angle from her hand, attached now only by skin and sinew.

Sweat ran down her cheek, traced her jaw, and trickled along her neck and chest. Her throat burned with her panting. She had no idea how much time had passed. The sun hung cold and motionless in the empty sky. The gray-green ocean surged and receded, uncaring. She squinted up the shoreline. Was the whale still there? It was.

Her legs trembled; she was *so* tired. But eager to be finished, eager to be free, she took up the knife again. It wasn't her arm, or any arm, really; this thing in front of her was nothing more than a useless, frayed rope that needed to be severed completely.

Eyeing the narrowest part of her wrist, she attacked. That, she discovered, was like trying to hack through seaweed with a spoon; though she pressed with all her might, the sinews were too tough. She couldn't do it. The cruel fact of the matter was that she'd gotten this far and yet she wasn't going to get free. The insects—and the ravens, too—would have their feast after all.

Blinded by anger, she lifted the knife in the air and slammed the point into her wrist. It plunged in with hardly any feeling whatsoever and she continued her work, sweat streaming from her face. Her breathing came in pinched gasps. Time and again the staggering pain swallowed her into blackness, and each time she awoke, the knife had clattered free of her hand.

Each instance was a struggle to remember where she was and what she had to do, but then she'd manage to retrieve the knife and return to her stabbing and tearing. When her arm—her good arm, anyway, and there was a strange thought, she'd always speak of her good arm now—grew weak, she rested, slumping against the rock, savoring the cold against her sweaty cheek, gazing up the beach at the whale like it was a prize. *What would you trade? What would you trade?* The mystifying words urged her on, and though her stomach upended in protest, she clenched her jaw and returned to her labor.

When her arm finally fell free, the pain that had stopped at her shoulder sent probing hot fingers racing through her chest to squeeze the air from her lungs. Already light-headed, she fought for breath. At once she turned from the grotesque sight of her mangled remnant of a wrist disappearing beneath the boulder. Insects swarmed hungrily, and she cradled the remainder of her arm. A wave of dizziness rocked her, and she let herself fall back against the bluff to keep from pitching forward into air. With her lone hand she worked her way beneath her dress and wriggled out of her underskirt. Icy winds licked her bare skin, but she didn't shiver. As best as she could, she wound the linen garment around her stumpy arm, wadding it tight against the profuse bleeding. That took all her energy, and she leaned against the bluff for another respite. She still had so far to go. How was she going to manage the rest of her descent with only one arm?

The ocean gusts continued to assail her. Their chill was welcomed now. It kept her sharp and attuned to the precarious task of a difficult descent. She moved slowly, careful to press her body to the bluff as she slid across each rock. As much as she tried to protect her throbbing limb, she seemed to knock it at every turn, and more than once she cried out before cradling it closer and continuing.

The ravens accompanied her; why, she didn't know. They swooped lazily through the air, their calls alternately joyous and then, when she moaned, alarmed. In a distant sort of way they provided comfort. When she neared the bottom, their chortles and trills got lost among the rushing surf and a persistent buzzing in her head. And an excited nicker.

A what? A nauseating fog clouded her mind. She blinked, forcing herself to stay alert. The familiar sound came again, from somewhere below. Leaning tight against the cliff, double-checking her balance, she dared to peer downward.

There on the shore, ears pricked in her direction, waited Rune.

XXVIII
TUTTUGU OK ÁTTA

Oh, it felt good! The warm current at the base of his furry coat. The smell of him, sweet and clean, peppered with sand, his breath grassy. She crumpled against his shoulder, aching to close her eyes until the middle of summer, at least. Dimly she felt his lips nuzzling concern along her head and neck. But sleep's soothing blanket was already wrapping her. The ocean was filling her ears with its whispers. She could allow herself a rest . . . just a short one . . . until . . .

And melting into the syrupy blackness, she felt herself drift away, felt herself falling . . . falling . . .

Falling!

Just in time she flailed her arms, planted her foot, and caught herself. What had happened? Where was she? Blinking, scrambling to gather her wits, she realized that Rune had stepped out from under her. In his own way he was eyeing her with disapproval. He snorted and shook his head. He pawed the sand and, from beneath his heavy forelock, delivered his most penetrating stare.

Of course. She couldn't sleep. Not right now, anyway, and not here. She had to get home—fast. Inhaling the cold, salty air—and gagging on its soggy weight—she tried to focus her thoughts. To get home, she had to find a way to mount.

The very idea of that held her in place, stupefied. Climbing onto Rune's back appeared at that moment as daunting as reclimbing the mountain she'd just descended. It just wasn't possible. Her arm hurt too much. Her legs had no strength. She couldn't.

But here was Rune, when she'd not even asked, folding his knees and dropping onto the sand with a sigh. It was the trick she'd taught him as a child—a lifetime ago.

Such selflessness! It squeezed her tight, made her eyes sting.

New resolve ignited within her. "All right," she croaked, sore-throated. (Was that *her* voice?) "If you can manage it with your bad leg, I can manage it with one arm." And ever so gingerly she maneuvered her right leg over him and settled onto his warm back, gripping his sides with her knees. How odd it felt, after having not sat in days. To protect her throbbing stump of a limb, she clamped it close to her chest, then grabbed a hank of mane. Could he, as old as he was, battle-weary and injured, manage to rise to his feet?

What if they both fell? Imagining the excruciating pain of slamming onto the hard sand stiffened her spine. Maybe she shouldn't—*No, no, no,* she scolded, forcing herself to relax. She could trust him. He was Rune.

Anxious, wondering, she nevertheless sat fixed. The ocean rushed and retreated, rushed and retreated. Rune remained kneeling. At long last he sucked in a deep breath, and with an explosive grunt extended his front legs. That raised his withers, and she leaned into the motion to keep her balance. He teetered there, legs splayed, then grunted again and heaved his hindquarters up to a shaky stance.

For a while she swayed atop a floundering ship. Rune struggled to walk a line, but each hobbling step sent him lurching first one way and then the other. He faded to a halt, trembling. His skin twitched with irritation. His ears flicked forward and back. He seemed to be thinking, to be mustering his own resolve, and it must have been so, for soon enough he struck out again, one hesitant step at a time, and they began making their way along the shore.

The blueish light of the fading day smudged her sight; it played tricks on her eyes and fogged her thinking. Everything sounded so loud inside her head: the surf, her breathing, the crunching sand. Without looking up she became aware of the two ravens accompanying them. Their jolting yelps pierced her skull until the buzzing already inside drowned them. Her arm's throbbing measured their progress—if you could call it that—for each hoof-heavy step was labored. Clearly Rune suffered as much pain as she, and she rubbed her gratitude into his withers.

The blackness continued to tug at her with such sweet promises that she frequently had to shake her head, twist her neck, and stretch her jaw just to stay awake. Luckily chilling gusts whipped the hair about her face and pushed her onward.

Dusk deepened to night, and the ravens' calls escalated from placid *quorks* to excited *kr-r-ucks!* They were calling to her now, calling her name. *Asa, Asa,* they encouraged, almost human.

"Asa! Asa!" So very human.

"Asa!" Through the deafening throb imprisoning her body she heard her name. And she recognized a voice: Wenda. Blinking, she lifted her head and tried to shake it clear. A yellow flame bobbed in the darkness. The splashing waves liquefied its brilliance and scattered its light across the shimmering water. Holding the flame high was a cloaked figure who waved a welcome and guided her home with shouts of joy: "You did it! You did it!"

"The whale," she mumbled thickly. "I found the whale."

"I'll send them for it," came the reply. "Your part is finished."

And then the hands again, lifting her down—Where was she? What was happening?—and the floor became the ceiling and the rafters ensnared her and the world spun top for bottom. More fire appeared, orange and snapping. She stared, entranced, unable to move. The many hands pressed upon her and pulled at her, and at one point the fire seemed to leap over to her and burn through her arm with its ferocious bite. She cried out, that much she knew, and her gaping mouth clamped down on a mug of steaming liquid that burned her lips. The taste on her tongue was oh-so-bitter and she tried to push it away but . . . but—Why wouldn't her hands obey?—the delicious blackness came flooding in, and this time she gave in and did let herself go falling . . . falling . . . falling.

XXIX TUTTUGU OK NÍU

Although the sea sent chill breezes gusting up the fjord, the sun warmed the damp earth around the village. Almost overnight a vibrant green had painted the strip of land squeezed between water and mountain.

Asa stood on a gentle rise beside the longhouse. Having considered all the possibilities, she dragged a stick to etch four lines in the mud. Yes, this would do. The site was high enough to catch a bit of wind to stoke the cooking fires, but near enough to the longhouse to easily carry the sizzling meats on their serving trays. Tora had been complaining for days that the hearth wasn't big enough for all the cooking and preserving they'd been doing, and when Ketil had reminded Asa that her father had promised a new cooking shed, she immediately stepped outside to select a location. It would be the first project under her reign as clan chieftain, and she wanted to make sure it was right. As Ketil watched, she moved about inside the imaginary walls she'd outlined, made one-handed motions of lighting a fire, of lifting bags from hooks, of chopping and stirring. Had she remembered everything? She frowned, thinking.

Along which wall would the water barrels sit? Well, she'd leave that to Tora. The woman needed to be mistress of something, and this cooking shed would serve nicely. Besides, useful work bred more loyalty than a silver ring pin.

Standing at her invisible doorway, she raised an eyebrow in Ketil's direction. He nodded. "It'll do. I'll have the boys start digging at once. Good day for it too," he added, lifting a cheek to the sunny sky. "First of many, I suspect." And with that he gave her his best smile.

She nodded in return. At one time she might have thrown her arms around his neck, but that was when she was just a girl; now she was clan chieftain. There were unspoken boundaries.

Stepping across the nascent threshold, she left Ketil to his work and climbed the path to the outfields. Along the stream, pristine white snowdrops shivered on their stems and the spicy fragrance of juniper scented the air.

The geese had returned seven days ago. Their trumpeting calls had awakened her before dawn, and she'd left her mattress to stand shivering in the gray light and watch their wavering V formation pass overhead. Finally . . . *finally* . . . summer had arrived!

In the nearer of the outfields Rune and the other two horses, each as thin as skeletons, busily nibbled their way across the new blades. They heard her approach—she could tell by the flicking ears—but only Rune lifted his head to whinny a greeting. His bristly, upright mane was already beginning to flop over, and he looked sadly comical as he limped toward her. But what a welcome sight. The day he'd rescued her, she was so weak and had lost so much blood that she doubted she'd have made it back to her clan. Again he'd saved her life. He butted her shoulder, begging for a treat, and she fed him a barley cake. For the rest of his days, she'd always carry these treats for her trusted friend.

A loud *gronk* shattered the morning, startling her. She would never get used to the capricious visits unique to Wenda's mischievous ravens.

"Ach, you keep sweetening him like that, and he'll be waddling like a goose before Shieling Month."

Asa shook her head. Nor would she get used to the way Wenda could seemingly appear from air. She turned to find the one-eyed woman smiling.

"But you can both do with a little fat on your ribs." Wenda handed Rune some more barley cakes and her a portion of *mylja*. How many days in a row had she bolted down the crumbly flatbread made so much better with melted whale blubber? Not enough to satisfy. Without hesitation she sank her teeth into it.

The old woman had settled in as the clan's skald. Well, "settled" wasn't exactly the right word, because she rarely sat for longer than the span of a story before rising and busying herself with some nonurgent task, regularly glancing toward the door or the ocean, as if she were expecting someone, or as if she, herself, were planning to flit away. But she'd brought bags of new stories to carry them through the summer nights, and she was relating them with an artful zeal that seemed to please her as well as the clan.

"How's the arm today?" The motherly concern in her voice warmed Asa.

"It hurts. And it's still keeping me awake nights. And sometimes"—this was rather unnerving—"sometimes when I lie really quiet I can feel my hand, though I know that's not possible."

Wenda nodded. "We always have a sense for what's been lost." She turned and gazed through the trees to the ocean, then stalked toward them, studiously avoiding the circle of ashes and charcoal where Jorgen's body had been burned. She gazed down toward the settlement, and Asa left Rune to join her.

Ketil already had Helgi and Thidrick digging a trench for the foundation. The two boys carefully followed the lines she'd scratched, and that gave her pride. Gunnvor emerged from the longhouse to watch, coaxing little Engli along at the end of her hand. It was the first time he'd been on his feet in a month. Yes, everything about the day—the generous sun, the construction of the cooking shed, the sparkle returning to Rune's eyes—heralded good fortune.

Without glancing over she felt Wenda's one eye boring into her. Though she'd related her trial in exhaustive detail to her clan, and answered so many questions that she'd finally held up her hand and forbidden more, she'd not discussed a word of it with Wenda. Oddly, it was she who'd had bandages and the bitter medicinal tea waiting that night. But now, at last, Asa sensed a question coming.

"Did you make a good trade?"

How many times she'd asked herself that same question! Especially those first days, passed writhing on her mattress in agonizing pain. Had she? Thoughtfully she studied the village below. Astrid and young Pyri were wringing out freshly laundered bedsheets. Tora was scraping remnants from one of the giant whale bones dragged closer to the longhouse. The door to the livestock byre stood propped open, and the cow ambled through the settlement at will, grazing in bliss. Her surviving calf skipped and played by its lonesome, exuberant as only one who was innocent of darker days could be.

Pride swelled her chest. Her clan was safe and, under her leadership, would remain so. They had food and warmth. They had each other. And now, for one sacrifice, they had hope. Her father and her mother both would have been proud.

A good trade? She lifted her face to the sun, closed her eyes, and nodded, smiling. "Yes," she answered. "A good trade."

AUTHOR'S NOTE

This novel began, oddly enough, as a picture book. I had envisioned pages of colorful illustrations depicting magnificent blue and green fjords, red Viking ships, golden ponies, and one very determined copper-headed girl named Asa. Since a nearby museum was hosting a special exhibit on Vikings, I began my research there.

Among the many artifacts on display I spied a carved antler comb that I imagined Asa using, a pointed spur she would never have needed with Rune, and a gold and silver brooch her mother might wear. Inspired, I picked up a few books at my local library and returned home. Then I wrote the first lines: "In the pale light of a wintry morning seven men saddled their ship across bucking white waves. A girl stood alone on the shore."

I kept on writing, but as much as I tried to compress Asa's story into a handful of illustration-friendly pages, she kept slipping off them and whispering that there was more to her life. Frustrated but intrigued, I set aside my wordy draft and followed.

I visited a larger public library and two university libraries to dig more deeply into the Viking culture. One of the first things

I learned was that the Vikings did NOT wear horned helmets! That's a modern myth. Yes, they were marauders; in fact, the very name *Viking* means to go forth and raid, to go "a-viking." But many times they were forced to set sail in search of land and food because the habitable areas around their fjords were too narrow to afford sufficient room for crops and livestock. This was especially true on the western coast of modern-day Norway where Asa's story takes place.

During the time that this book was bursting free of its picture book bindings, I had the opportunity to visit Scotland and England, areas of which were once settled by Vikings. At the Royal Museum of Scotland I discovered a hammered metal helmet crafted by a Viking for a warrior pony, a helmet with the most magnificent curling horns. I knew Asa had a very special horse and became certain he would have worn this exact helmet—until I read the tiny museum note card stating that while experts had also once been excited by this find, all had determined that the helmet was an example of a nineteenth-century reconstructive error. Okay, okay. Not even the Viking horses had horned helmets.

In the beautiful English walled city of York I toured the Jorvik Viking Centre. Stationed upon an ongoing archaeological dig, this museum has unearthed more than forty thousand Viking objects, and among the many on display were shoes and clothing more than a thousand years old. Amazing. Also at Jorvik I got to experience a life-size recreation of a Viking settlement—complete with sounds and smells—which provided invaluable research material.

Time and again I came across depictions of Viking mythology: Thor's hammer, Freyr's golden boar, the Valkyries with their offering cups. But the god that intrigued me most was the mercurial, one-eyed Odin. A seeker of knowledge, Odin could change his shape at will, and in some accounts traveled as a woman on a white horse. He had sacrificed his eye in exchange for wisdom—sacrifice for the greater good being a revered attribute and common theme in Viking mythology—but continued to seek understanding, often ordering his two ravens to bring him news of the world. I wanted him to be part of Asa's story and therefore modeled the enigmatic Wenda after him, creating her name to reflect Odin's nickname, "the wanderer."

In my reading I learned how important storytelling was to passing long winters in tight quarters. (Perhaps because the winters were so long, the Vikings had names for only two seasons: summer and winter.) The skald—or storyteller—was highly respected, second only to the clan chieftain, and if he could interpret runes (the carved symbols that served as an alphabet) he was thought to possess almost magical powers. So what would a silver-tongued skald bubbling with evil ambition do with such powers? And how does an entranced audience sift truth from fact?

I was surprised to discover that the Vikings were fairly egalitarian. Men and women could each own property and could have a say in how things were run, and if a man went off to battle, a woman could run the clan in his place. I learned that self-sufficiency was much admired and that an independent spirit in children—even to the point of being outspoken and argumentative—was encouraged. That's when Asa finally nodded, stepped back, and allowed me to tell her story.

As she makes her extraordinary leap from young woman to clan leader, Asa struggles with the sacrifices required of good leaders, and she gradually learns to balance the needs of the community against those of the individual—challenging tasks for anyone. But as her father pronounced at her birth, Asa is "no ordinary child," and her story exceeds the bounds of pictures.